Growing Home

a novel

Growing Home
A Novel

Schreiner, Jane S., Author
Growing Home
Jane S. Schreiner

ISBN 978-1492109020

1. Women's Fiction

Book Design and Cover Design © 2013

Growing Home

a novel

Jane S. Schreiner

DEDICATION

Growing Home is dedicated to the first great
teacher and comfort provider in my life,
Rosemary Susan Sampson.
You're still the one I turn to Mom.
I love you forever.

Acknowledgments

First I want to acknowledge Robin Colucci Hoffmann, my writing coach. This book simply would not have happened without your endless teaching and critique. We had a special partnership. Thank you.

Next are my greatest blessings, my children Frank Sampson Grundler, Susan Currans Grundler, Sammy Beth Schreiner, Ellie Jane Schreiner. I thank God everyday for letting me be your Mother. Thank you for choosing to get here through me. You are each an unspeakable gift in my life. Bless you all.

And my daughter-in-law, Miriam Meima, the newest gift to our family. Love and smiles surround you. Thank you for coming in to our lives.

Life always provides what we need, if we are open to seeing it. Greg Schreiner has truly been a teacher to me. Thank you for the lessons we have learned together, in countless ways. I love you always.

To my father Harold Y. Sampson for his emotionally intelligent support of me, whenever I need it. You're a special man Dad. I treasure you.

To my sister and brother-in-law, Ann and Eric Fetsch for their light, love and unconditional support. Such a gift! I love you.

To my brother and his family, Henry, Daphne, Sabrina and Anthony Sampson. You all make me smile and share you support with the most fun and joy! I adore each of you.

To my sister, friend and baby steps coach, Teresa Schreiner. One step at a time! Love always...

To Susan Appel McQuiston, 48 years of watching each other grow and strive to be our best selves. What a ride! Love and hugs, friend.

To Kim Gibler for believing in me, and expressing that with the most beautiful words. Thank you sweet friend. You are priceless to me.

To my dear YIT, Allison Grenney, your partnering and support are indispensable to me! You are a great blessing in my life.

And for the greatest guide and mentor in my life, always there, no matter what, Carolyn Braddock. Bless you my precious friend. You have always known when to suggest, when to wait and when to push. Thank God.

Chapter One

The barn was a good place to be on a hot August afternoon. It was cooler there, especially in the storeroom tucked under the hayloft. I laid out a pillowcase to form a temporary altar and smoothed it out over the dirt floor. My hands got sweaty as I turned the old fishbowl upside down to make a crystal ball. I set it in the middle of the altar, right next to the candles that were already dripping wax onto the cat dish.

"Tommy, settle down. Grandpa is out working...and Boone too."

He glanced over his shoulder to the storeroom door. "This is crazy, Mary. What do I have to do?"

"All you have to do is hold hands with me and think about my momma while I ask her to come. Like the séance on TV."

"How can I do that when I never knew your momma?"

"Tommy, come on, please try. This'll work, I know it will."

Tommy looked unconvinced but held my hands anyway.

"Now quit fidgeting or you'll knock over the candles." She steadied his hands, "Let's start."

Facing each other, we raised our joined hands over the upside-down fishbowl and the candles sitting on the cat dish.

"Momma, it's Mary. Please come to us. It's okay, Grandpa won't know. I need you, Momma, and I miss you so much. Please come so we can see you."

Nothing happened at first, so I called her again. The air shifted and goose bumps popped out on my arms. The calico jumped down from the hay pile and we nearly fell over.

Shaken, Tommy said, "That's it Mary. This is dumb."

"No, no, please stay for just one more try. I know this is going to work, and you know how much I need to reach my momma. Come on, okay?"

Exasperated, he took his seat again as I straightened everything just so. "Sorry Momma. That was the cat, but you probably know that. Now, please come and let me see you…"

We heard a bang followed by the clattering of metal on concrete, out in the barn. There was a stirring again and the door came open a little. I was sure I saw smoke swirl in the bowl, like it did on TV, but that was it. Tommy hopped to his feet.

"I'm sorry, but I can't do this anymore. I'll meet you at the pond," and he zipped out of there.

I stared at the door Tommy had left through. The room turned cold, and my gaze shifted back to the bowl. There she was, a beautiful, dark-haired lady gazing tenderly at the baby in her arms. She looked up and smiled at me through the bowl, but her eyes seemed sad.

✺

My Grandpa Gerald was the only family I had ever known. Dorothy Freeman too, she was our neighbor and like a Grandma to me I guess. She and her daughter Maddie had always been a part of my life. Since my father was killed in the Korean War before I was born, and my mother died when I was an infant, I had been an orphan. I was a headstrong sort of girl—at least that's what Grandpa said. The summer before I turned ten I had a hunger to know about my roots, to know more about my momma. Grandpa never would talk about her; I guess it was too hard for him to go back and look at memories of his only child. But I wasn't thinking about that then; I was on a quest. I felt a need to talk to her, to know her and to feel like she was with me.

That summer, my only friend, Tommy, and I spent most of our time at the pond. Summers in Missouri are hot and muggy, which was the main reason the pond was our favorite place. We spent hours catching fish with nothing more than long sticks, fishing line, and hooks squirming with night crawlers. Catching frogs kept us busy too. We usually had them for supper, but one time I kept one of the frogs for company. I used a shoebox, poked air holes in the top of it, and gave the frog bugs to eat. It wasn't long before I felt bad about keeping it locked up like that. I took off the top, and for a minute, the frog just sat there, sensing the change in the air flow and figuring out that freedom was just one big hop away. Finally, he jumped out and I was amazed at how high he was able to jump.

One morning late in August 1963, I woke up thinking about my birthday the following week. A warm breeze came through the window above my head, and the curtain puffed out over my face. It felt familiar and comforting. Turning ten was exciting and having two numbers in my age, well it was a big leap in feeling grown up.

With thoughts of Tommy coming over that morning to meet me at the pond, I hopped right up to do my chores. First, I was off to the barn to milk our two cows and clean out their stalls. Next, I had to empty the milk into the cooler and put Bessie and Bedelia out in the pasture.

Grandpa was already in the barn when I got there.

"Good morning," he said. "When you're done with those cows, go on back to the house. There are some chores to do there before you can go to the pond with Tommy."

"Yes, Grandpa," I said, not feeling like I wanted to do any of that. No matter how I felt, though, I always said yes to my grandpa. He was a quiet man, a good man. He had a calm, gentle voice and smelled of shaving cream.

"Oh, and check to be sure we have candles in case a birthday comes along sometime soon." That made me smile. I knew it was his way of letting me know that he remembered my birthday was coming up the next week. Maybe he had something special planned this year, like going to town for ice cream and letting me get all the penny candy I wanted. Or maybe I could get the doll I had seen at the five-and-dime. Her name was Chatty Cathy, and when I first saw her I was captivated. I picked her up and realized she talked when you pulled the string, and I was "over the moon" with the idea of having her come live with me. That had been the previous Christmas, which seemed like forever ago. I imagined playing with her in my room and sleeping with her every night. I was thinking about all of that as I left the barn and made patterns in the dust with the toe of my boot, none too anxious to get the house chores done.

As I worked, I picked up my pace a little. I had a plan to go back out to the barn when I was done. There was something I wanted to check out that I'd noticed some days before, up in the loft. I already knew that we had birthday candles, because I had a couple hidden with my séance things in the barn. Grandpa Gerald said the loft was off limits, so I had to sneak up there, which is what I'd done a few days earlier when I was snooping around the barn. That's when I first saw something that looked like it could be a trunk, but I barely got a glimpse before I heard Grandpa's truck pull up outside, and I had to scramble back down the ladder.

Grandpa wasn't around, so I ventured up the loft ladder again, just far enough to peek over the edge and look around. Sure enough, there was an old trunk close to the hay loading doors.

I wonder what's inside that thing, I thought.

I heard Grandpa Gerald coming, so I hurried back down the ladder and picked up a rake. He came into the barn and seemed surprised to find me there.

"I was just finishing cleaning the stalls. I didn't think I got it well enough earlier, so I wanted to finish up."

"Well, that's good, but you know I don't like you in here alone. Come on now, it's good enough."

"Okay. Can I go down to the pond and see if Tommy is there yet? We were talking about swimming this morning."

"Sure, you go on now. I'll see you back in time for dinner. How 'bout fixing up some ham sandwiches today?"

"I'll have them ready when you come in from working."

I ran off down the hill toward the pond. It was a gentle slope covered with deep green grass, and I had worn a path along it from going back and forth over the years. This was my life, and other than feeling curious about my momma, I liked it.

When I got to the pond, Tommy was already there, swimming in the water. I had my swimming suit with me, and I ducked into the trees to put it on. I came running out to the swing and jumped, grabbing ahold of the rope. Before Tommy could see I was coming, I dashed back up the hill, holding the rope, and ran right back down so I could push myself off and swing out over the water. *Splat!*

"Mary, what are you doing? You almost fell right on my head?"

"Well, why didn't you get out of the way?" I laughed.

As we swam that morning, I told him about climbing up the loft ladder. He knew I wasn't supposed to do that.

"What are you thinking? You could get in a lot of trouble."

"Aw, that rule is for babies. I can take care of myself. That ladder isn't such a big deal...and guess what? I saw a trunk on the front wall by the hay doors. I think we should go up there and see what it is and what's inside. Why don't you stay to dinner and then we can go up there after and take a look?"

"If your grandpa catches us, we'll be in big trouble. I don't want to get in trouble with him."

"He'll be back to work in the orchard. He'll never know."

He finally gave in. "But you promise me we'll go up and come right back down?"

I nodded.

He paused, "Why do I always let you talk me into this stuff?"

"'Cause you know I'm right. We've never gotten in any bad trouble with Grandpa before. It won't take us long to see what's there. We'll be quick about it, I promise."

After noon dinner, Grandpa was out the door with a thank you and back to work. Tommy helped me clean up, and I hurried us along to get out to the barn. I couldn't let him see that I was nervous or he would have chickened out.

I said, "Last one to the barn is a rotten egg!" He was

on the porch and down the steps in no time.

Following right behind him I said, "Let's go around to the side door." It was a good way to sneak into the barn because it was hard to see from any direction. The big gas tank was by there and blocked the door from view. It was eerily quiet in the barn. *Probably just my jitters*, I thought, but since I was determined, we made a beeline for the ladder. I went first.

Tommy hesitated, "Come on Tommy, start climbing."

It took him a minute, and then he started climbing up behind me. I got to the top and peered over the edge of the loft floor, just to be sure there wasn't anything moving around up there. You never knew what you might find running across the floor. Could be a coon or mice or rats. You just never knew. But it was all clear, and I climbed up onto the loft floor.

I called down to him, "What's taking you so long? You're barely climbing the ladder."

"Geez, the stuff I do for you," and he got moving then. At the top of the ladder, I pointed out what I was talking about.

"See the hayloft doors? The trunk's to the left there. You can see the end sticking out behind the hay bales and corral panels."

We couldn't see it very clearly. Guess that's why I'd never noticed it before when I'd been up there with Grandpa.

"Come on, let's go and check it out." I grabbed ahold of his hand. It was sweaty. We walked carefully around some of the stuff so we could get to the far side by the loft doors. It was a long drop down to the barn floor, and there weren't any railings or anything else to keep us from going over the edge, so we were extra alert.

Tommy said, "Yeah, it's definitely a trunk." We could see it more clearly now. There were some hay bales to climb over still but we could see it.

"Oh, it might be my momma's!" We scrambled over the hay bales, and there it was, sitting alone by itself against the wall. I stopped for a second, caught in anticipation of what we might find. I was suspended there, with a knowing that my life was about to change.

"Come on, what are you waiting for?" Tommy jarred me from my thoughts.

I walked up to the trunk and felt it with my hands. Covered in dust, it had a rounded top from front to back that got tall in the middle. The old lock hung loose as I struggled to lift the heavy lid. Tommy joined me, using both hands to help.

Reverently the inside revealed itself, lined with cream-colored paper covered in little violets, like wallpaper. The floral paper was even on the inside of the lid. As I took in the contents of the trunk, I saw that it held layers of things all wrapped in tissue paper. I picked up the first thing I saw and gingerly unwrapped it. As the paper unfolded, a beautiful picture of my momma appeared. I could barely breathe. I hadn't seen many pictures of her, but I knew it was my momma. Holding a baby that must have been me, she looked tired and thin. She couldn't have been very old in this photo, since she was only twenty-four when she died, and Mrs. Freeman said that had been too young to die. As I carefully lifted the picture out, I was mesmerized by the sight of her and how loving she looked. I hugged her photo close to me. Such a fine silver frame, with fancy silver flowers all around the edge. I wanted to be extra careful with it. I felt my momma, felt her right there all around me, and this is what I had longed for. As I turned and laid the picture on the hay bale behind me, I was caught by the sweetest smell of flowers. I closed my eyes for just a moment to take it all in, and it felt like heaven.

I turned back to the trunk and started to lift up more layers to uncover what was underneath. I forgot everything but what I was seeing. Under the paper was a present. I didn't understand that. *Why would there be a present wrapped with birthday cake paper and a pink bow?*

Just then, we heard Grandpa's truck pull up outside the barn. As he slid open the big door right below where we were standing in the loft, he hollered to someone that he would be right out. Tommy and I froze where we were, holding so still that we almost forgot to breathe.

I heard Grandpa rustling around his tool bench. He was obviously looking for something. We glanced at each other, knowing we shared the same hope that he'd find it and leave. As I held real still and wondered what was next, Grandpa made a banging noise and called out to his long time farm hand, "I found it, Boone." The sound of his footsteps, followed by the smooth glide of the big doors sliding closed, were our cue that we were back in business.

I held my finger in front of my lips until we heard

the engine start and the truck drive off. Then we both began talking at once.

"We better get out of here," we said at the same time.

"He might come back," Tommy said.

"But what do you make of this present in here?" I asked as I looked again inside the trunk.

"I don't know, Mary, but we better go now and figure it out later."

"Alright, help me close this lid. It's heavy."

Tommy obliged.

"Promise you will come back with me soon," I said. "I have to see what else is in here. I need a closer look at that present too. I wonder who it's for."

As we turned to leave, I grabbed the picture and put it down the front of my coveralls. It practically filled the whole space. I had to push it tight in to the waist so it wouldn't slide out as I climbed down the ladder.

We left through the side door and looked around to make sure Grandpa was really gone. He was, so Tommy and I ran to the house. Tommy waited downstairs while I went up to my room. I used the chair by my door to climb up in the closet and get the blanket I used in winter for extra covers when it got really cold. Once I got the picture wrapped up good and snug in that old blanket, I put the bundle up on the closet shelf and pushed the chair back over by the door.

As I walked back into the kitchen, Tommy said, "Let's go swimming again, okay? I just want to go swing over the water and maybe do some fishing."

"Okay, let's go. But remember you promised we will go back to the loft soon. I want to do another séance, too, especially now that we found Momma's picture. We can use that, you know."

He shrugged and said, "Let's go."

"Did you smell the flowers up in the loft?"

His look was quizzical, "What flowers? What are you talking about?"

That was curious, I thought, *I guess he didn't smell them.* "Never mind, let's go."

Later that night when I was cleaning the supper dishes, all I could think about was the trunk in the loft. I said goodnight to Grandpa Gerald early, while it was still light outside and the late-day stillness had settled in on us. Going up to my room, I was thinking of my new treasure.

I couldn't wait to see the picture again. I moved the chair to the closet so I could get the blanket down. Then "*bump.*" I accidentally knocked it against the closet doorframe and Grandpa hollered up the stairs, "What's going on up there?"

"Nothing, Grandpa, I'm just cleaning my closet shelves a little."

My nerves sure were getting a workout. I waited a second and he didn't say anything else. I retrieved the blanket and unwrapped the frame, setting it on my old braided rug. There was a stand attached in the back, and I stood the frame up where I could look right at it. Next, I got my picture collection out of the shoebox that was in my bottom dresser drawer. Inside, there was a photo of me when I was really little.

Mrs. Freeman was holding my hand and walking beside me. I had a dress on. I hardly wore dresses except for church on Easter Sunday, so this must have been taken one Easter. Then, there was another one, of me in the school Christmas pageant as the Mother Mary, when I was in second grade. I remembered how the pageant confused me. My real name was Mary, but I was pretending to be Mary, the mother of Jesus. I didn't get that. On my 8th birthday, as I blew out the candles with Grandpa Gerald and Tommy at the table watching, Mrs. Freeman had taken a picture of me then too. That photo was in my box as well.

I'd been on a high all day, ever since we'd been in the loft that morning, but now that odd, empty feeling came over me again as I looked at my pictures. I missed my Momma. I felt the longing so plainly that my eyes got all teary. Sitting cross legged there on the rug, with pictures all around me, and I got lost in imagining what it would have been like to have my momma to take care of me and hug me every day. Thinking about that was almost too hard. I wanted her so much. I leaned back against the bed and closed my eyes, imagining my tenth birthday the following week with her baking me a cake and wrapping a present just for me—maybe even making me a present, something really special. I was captivated by the scene, getting lost in the imagining.

I must have fallen asleep because it was dark when I woke up later, all curled up on the rug with pictures still around me. It took me a minute to realize where I was, and then I remembered what I had been doing before I fell asleep. I sat back up and looked out the window over my bed. The moon was shining into my room and a light breeze was making the curtain flutter.

It was cooler, but just a little better than earlier in the evening.

I got up off the floor gathering my pictures. It must have been close to the time of the full moon, because the light shining through my window was bright enough for me to see around my room. I carefully put the pictures back into the shoebox, and this time I put the one of Momma and me in there too. The framed photo fit in the box when I laid it at an angle on its side. I opened the top drawer and got my pajamas out. My drawer was squeaky and hard to open and because I didn't want to wake up Grandpa, I opened it slowly. He didn't like for me to be awake so late. Grandpa always said, "The early bird catches the worm, and you can't get up early if you stay up late." I knew I should brush my teeth, but that might wake him so I got into bed instead. The fresh smell of clean sheets made settling in feel so good and cozy. I put my head on the pillow and breathed it in.

Going back to sleep wasn't easy. I lay there on my back, watching the shadows on the wall at the foot of my bed. A big maple tree creaked outside my window, the branches made dancing shadows as the wind started to blow harder. For what seemed like a long time, I watched those shadows sway.

The next morning was Saturday, only two days away from my birthday, and I was excited. Saturday was our go-to-town day, the day set aside for shopping and errands. But on that Saturday before my birthday, I got to thinking—I could just stay home. Mrs. Freeman would watch me while Grandpa was gone. Then Tommy and I could sneak back into the barn and hold another séance with my newly-found picture of Momma.

That brought me right up and out of bed. I put my coveralls back on from the day before and took a clean t-shirt from the dresser. *I think I feel like wearing the blue one today,* I thought. I loved blue, and the day felt like it was going to be a really good one.

When I got to the kitchen for breakfast, Grandpa already had my cereal bowl out.

"Hey, sleepy head," he said, "you're up kind of late..." *Whoops*, I thought, *it's already 7:00 and we usually have breakfast at 6:00.*

"I let you sleep in a little, and I've got the milking all done. I need to go to town for supplies, and it looks like we need groceries from the Kroger's too. I thought you might want to stay home and spend some time with Mrs. Freeman. She mentioned something about baking today, and I know how you like to help with that."

"That would be great," I said. *Wow, this was going to be easier than I thought.* "Are you sure you don't mind going to town alone?"

"I need to see Mr. Stanley at the feed store. Might even have a cup of coffee with him and visit awhile. You can go on over to Mrs. Freeman's as soon as you're done with the dishes. She said Tommy could come too. She's probably already got bread in the oven by now, and you can help her roll out those cinnamon rolls that we like so much."

"Okay, I'll call Tommy and tell him to meet me

there. I'll be sure to bring you back some rolls too." That made him smile.

I gave Grandpa Gerald a hug around the waist. He was a big man, and I could just barely get my arms around his sides.

"See you later, Grandpa."

I called Tommy and left a message to come on to Mrs. Freeman's. His momma said he was out doing chores and that she would tell him when he came back. As Grandpa Gerald drove away, I went to the sink to finish up the dishes. As soon as I could see he was gone, I darted back upstairs to get my new picture. I wrapped it in a t-shirt and ran to the barn to hide it in the store-room.

My mind was going so fast. *Tommy and I can come over here in a little while and have a séance with the picture. That'll be something for sure. I know we can make contact with Momma.* That's what they called it on TV, making contact.

I put the frame between a hay bale and the far wall, down on the floor with the bowl and the rest of our séance stuff.

When I got to Mrs. Freeman's, she was working on the dough for cinnamon rolls. "Come on in Mary and help me roll this out, will you please?"

Mrs. Freeman was the nicest lady in the whole world. No matter what, she always said please and thank you. She smiled a lot too, and I felt warm and peaceful around her.

"Sure, Mrs. F." That's what I called her. "I told Grandpa I would bring him some rolls."

She smiled, "Why, that's just what I had in mind. He loves them."

"Yes ma'am, he sure does, and I do too," I said with a smile. "Tommy will be coming to help us in a little while. He had to do chores first."

"It's always nice to have you two come around and help me on baking day."

The kitchen got hot in the summertime, but we didn't mind. We got to lick the bowl when we made frosting and sometimes we ate the cookie dough when Mrs. F made chocolate chip cookies. That was the best.

"Mrs. F, you know don't you, that it's almost my birthday?" Of course she knew, but I wanted to bring it up.

"Sure is. I remember the day you were born. You came before you were expected and there was a big fuss getting your momma to the hospital. I think I've told you this story before..."

"Will you please tell me again?" I asked. "I love hearing that story."

"Of course," she said as she started cutting the rolled-up dough into strips.

"It was a Wednesday. I remember because I was in the middle of putting up early apples and I usually can mid-week. Anyway, your grandpa called up on the phone, pretty worked up, and told me that Celia wasn't feeling too good. Well, your Grandpa is usually real calm so my ears perked up. He asked if I could come over, which, of course, I did. Your momma's labor pains were already coming fast and strong when I got to your house. I could see straightaway that you were ready to be born, and I told your grandpa that, too. 'Gerald, Celia is getting ready to have this baby,' I said. 'You need to pull the truck around and get her to the hospital.'"

"Your grandpa was as nervous as a cat. He liked to have flown out that door; he was in such a hurry."

"We got your momma into the truck and off they went. You were born only a few hours after they got to the hospital. Your grandpa called later, as excited as I'd ever heard him, to tell me that you were a girl and that Celia had named you Mary, after your grandma. It sure was a happy day."

"When did you first get to see me?"

"Well, Celia brought you home three days later. Your pa had only been gone a few months when you were born. He was a very brave soldier fighting for our country over in Korea, and we lost him in The Battle of Pork Chop Hill. We lost a lot of our boys in that battle. That was a very hard time for Celia, and she had barely smiled since she'd gotten the news. When I saw her come home and get out of the truck holding you, I remember thinking, *her smile is back*. That smile just lit up her whole face! It was a great relief to see her like that, Mary. And it was having you that brought the light back to her eyes."

I turned somber then and I got a flutter in my stomach but I had to ask, "How did Momma die, Mrs. F? Grandpa never wants to talk about it and I'm always wondering."

"Mary, your momma got very sick when you were

just four months old. You came to us right at the beginning of apple harvest, late that summer. By Thanksgiving, Celia seemed to have gotten the flu. As Christmas was coming, she was busy making things for you. She was so excited about your first Christmas. You know your red-and-white baby quilt? She made that for you then...and your Christmas stocking too. As December went by and Christmas came around, Celia still wasn't feeling well. The doctor told her to rest more but she wouldn't listen. By January, I went with her to the doctor again and he wanted your momma to go to Springfield to have some tests done. So your grandpa took her and you stayed with me. You were rolling over by then and trying to sit up. Just the cutest little thing, you were."

"The tests showed that your momma was very sick. She had leukemia, which is a kind of cancer. It was the same thing that took your Grandma Mary. Celia was with us five more months. During that time, she worked feverishly on a special gift for you. Maddie came back home from Springfield during that time. Mark and Emmy were just little tykes and it was a handful, but she wanted to be with your momma as much as she could, since they had been best friends their whole lives. We were at your house a lot, taking care of you and your momma. Watching you learn to sit up and crawl was the very best part of all our days, especially your momma's. You were the light in her eyes, Mary."

Right then I wanted to tell Mrs. F about the séances. How I knew Momma was still around and wanted to make contact with me. But something stopped me, and then Tommy came knocking at the back door.

"Hi Mary, hi Mrs. F!" Tommy called Mrs. Freeman Mrs. F just like me.

"Hi, Tommy," she said. "Come on over here and help me sprinkle cinnamon on this dough, will you please? We need to get the first pan of rolls into the oven."

"Will we be making cookies too?" Tommy asked while stepping in to help sprinkle the cinnamon.

Mrs. F checked the kitchen clock. "I think next week will be cookies. Mary and I have been so busy talking that I lost track of time." She winked at me. "With bread already baking and rolls going in next, I think that will fill all of our time for today."

I spoke up next, "We have some things to do around the pond anyway. Right, Tommy?"

Tommy looked at me quizzically, and then he seemed to get it.

"Oh, right, okay…next week for cookies." He sounded both resigned and disappointed.

We stayed a while longer as the rolls baked and Mrs. F gave us each a nice big slice of warm, freshly baked bread slathered with butter and her homemade grape jelly. She wrapped up a pan of cinnamon rolls for Grandpa and said we could go on out and play.

"Check in with me in a few hours, if your grandpa isn't back by then. Go on now." She smiled at us.

Tommy's boot sent rocks skittering ahead of us, and I was bursting with plans for our séance, "Let's go right to the barn. I know we'll reach Momma this time because now we have the picture frame and we can have the séance by the trunk. That's sure to be the best place for Momma, with her things all there, don't you think?" I was thinking of the flower smell too, but I didn't say that.

"I guess so. But can we be quick about this? It's hot and I want to go to the pond."

"Oh sure, we'll go swimming just as soon as we're all done. There will be a lot of time left."

When we got to the barn I opened the door to the familiar smells of hay and cattle. The cooler barn air welcomed me as I went into the storeroom and gathered our things to take up the ladder. The anticipation had me skittering about as I was anxious to get set up as quickly as possible. Momma would surely be waiting to visit with us.

With the pillowcase and candles stuffed in the bowl I made my way up the ladder. Tommy was already over by the trunk.

"It's a little tight here. I shoved this bale over all I could."

We had enough space on the floor to set up the bowl on the pillowcase. I didn't have the cats' dish, because I'd left it in the storeroom for them, so I dripped a little wax on the floor to hold the candles in place. I set the picture frame right in front of the trunk. The hinges creaked when we lifted up the top. I wasn't too worried about noise since I knew we were alone.

"I think Momma will be more likely to come to us with the lid up. It seems like her power is in here with her things."

We sat down on the floor, facing each other. I lit the candles and Tommy and I reached across and held hands. He didn't like that very much, but that's how they did it on TV, so we had to do it too.

Then I started talking, "Momma, please let us know that you are here. Please give me a sign. I miss you so much."

We were squeezed between the trunk and some hay bales. Tommy started complaining that he was getting too hot.

"Tommy, *shhh*. You have to concentrate or this won't work."

I had the bowl turned upside down, but there weren't any pictures or smoke in it.

I said again, "Please Momma, just give us a sign that you hear me." I opened one eye and saw that Tommy's eyes were wide open. He was looking around at everything and not concentrating at all. I whispered, "Close your eyes, Tommy. That will make it work better."

And that's when the wind kicked up and blew the loft doors all the way open. I knew it was Momma letting me know she was there. I squeezed Tommy's hands, thinking about how slippery they were. Then I smelled smoke. The thrill of that moment quickly became confusion as I opened my eyes and saw that the candles had blown over into a bale of hay. The fire was already taking hold on that bale. The loft was especially hot and dry and hay was quick to light. The wind blowing through the doors was making it worse. The next bale caught fire right away, and we were trapped. The way we had come. from the ladder was blocked by burning bales. We tried to put the fire out. Tommy grabbed the pillowcase and flipped the bowl right on my foot as he used it to smother the flames, but it was no use. The fire was spreading too fast. The stack of bales behind me was almost as high as the ceiling so we couldn't climb out that way either. Our only chance was to jump down into the barnyard, but that was a long way down. I reached into the trunk and grabbed the present that was sitting close to the top. We were stepping on the picture frame so I picked that up too. Tommy was already standing at the doors yelling that we needed to get out of there. The smoke was thick. I stood next to him at the edge and yelled, "How do we do this, Tommy? It's too far to jump!"

That's when Grandpa Gerald drove up in his truck, the back loaded to the top with grain. He scrambled out of the cab and in a clear, firm voice said, "Mary, you jump first into the back of the truck. Then, Tommy you come right after her. Now, jump!"

I held tight to the treasures in my arms and jumped. It was a hard landing but better than hitting the dirt. Tommy came right after me and landed badly on his ankle. Grandpa got back in the truck and drove it over by the house, away from the barn. Getting out of the truck again and heading toward the barn, he ordered Tommy and me into the house.

"I have to go and save the barn."

"I'm coming with you," I announced.

"No, Mary!" Grandpa hollered. "You go inside and call Tommy's pa and Mrs. Freeman. Call the fire department, too."

Tommy couldn't get out of the truck with his injured ankle. Grandpa Gerald ran back to the barn and went inside. The wind had shifted, and the smell of smoke was filling my head. I left Tommy in the truck and ran to the phone in the house. Just as Mrs. F answered, I heard an awful explosion and I knew right away what had happened. The gas tank outside of the barn had exploded. I dropped the phone and ran out of the house, shocked by the force of heat and wall of flames coming from the barn.

"Grandpa, Grandpa!" I screamed. I ran around the barn to see if I could get in through the back door but no luck, so I went to the side door and there was smoke and fire everywhere. I pulled on the door, never noticing the pain in my hand. The door gave way and flames and heat rushed out at me. As I fell back, Mrs. Freeman came around the side of the barn and pulled me away just in time. The barn wall collapsed and fell into the side corral. I was screaming and crying hysterically for my grandpa. Tommy's dad drove up just then, saying the fire engine would be there soon.

"Where's your grandpa, Mary?" he shouted. "Where's Gerald?"

I was frantic to get Grandpa out of the barn. But it was too late. The barn was coming down and burning pieces were falling everywhere. Tommy's dad went for the hose, trying to spray his way into the barn to get to Grandpa. It was no use; the fire was out of control. The heat, smoke, and flames had won. I saw Tommy's dad stumble and fall, holding on to that hose with both hands, trying to get to my grandpa and save him.

It was all like a slow-motion nightmare—Tommy limping as he tried to help his dad; Mrs. F holding me so I wouldn't run into the barn, hugging me to her, crying; the fire engine pulling in and the men running around, hooking something up to the water tank in the corral, pointing hoses at the barn as water shot up high into the air. And there I was, screaming, knowing that my grandpa was gone. Gone, like Momma. Gone, on account of me—I had done exactly what he had told me not to do. Momma's things were gone too. My momma, my grandpa, and all Momma's pretty things in the trunk. All gone. I had nothing left and I wanted to die, too. I knew I should die for what I had done. That's what I knew.

Chapter Two

It's hard to remember what happened right after that. I am told that Dorothy, Mrs. F, took me home with her that day, and with the help of other folks, she handled the funeral and everything that needed to be done. She took care of me, my burned hand, and my broken heart. Poor Tommy broke his ankle when we jumped from the hay loft. He still favors that ankle to this day.

I have little memory from that time. Fall became winter, and then came the early spring. As the earth was awakening and growing new life, I too began to awaken fully from the pain I hadn't been able to bare. My first clear memory is on a soft spring day. I smelled the dampness from the remainders of fall's blanket of leaves that covered the ground and saw the early shoots of spring flowers peaking through them. I sat in a quiet little ravine under a grove of big oak trees just down the road from Mrs. F's house, all tucked in, with a hand-made quilt around me, the present that I had pulled from the trunk—the present Momma had been working on for me in those months before she died.

She had wrapped it up all pretty and asked Mrs. F and Grandpa to be sure I got the quilt for my tenth birthday. When I learned that, well, my heart nearly broke again. It seems she knew this was going to be a time when I especially needed her. She had made that beautiful quilt from pieces of all her favorite things through the years. I found the letter she'd written to me tucked in the folds.

"Mary, my sweet baby girl, I love you so much. You will be a big girl of ten when you read this. I am so sorry not to be there for you. When you feel lonely, wrap yourself up in this quilt and feel my love holding you tight. Feel your family all around you too, all of our good people who have come before and love you so much. I remember when I was your age how important family was for me. Each square of your quilt is a special message of love and support—the pieces of Grandpa's old shirts, my Ma's favorite apron patch, which once belonged to your Great Great Grandma Gert."

There was a piece of her own momma's favorite blouse, "The one with the lavender flowers," and a square made from the kerchief that Momma wore most days she worked around the house. She said it wasn't the prettiest fabric but had the most of her in it. There was also a square from one of my pa's shirts.

My whole family was in that quilt and Dorothy knew all about it. When I was in such a bad way after the fire and there was no way to celebrate my tenth birthday, Dorothy opened it with me. I don't remember it, but she read the letter to me and wrapped the quilt around me. She knew that it would comfort me and help me heal. She was right. The faint smell of Momma and the feel of my family close made the perfect healing gift.

I sat in the ravine, squatting and rocking back and forth on my heels. I remember watching a beetle make its way over some dead leaves and twigs. It was working so hard to get to where it was going. I felt that way, too, only I didn't know where I was going or why I would try. I remember feeling stuck, like I was trying to pull my feet from quicksand. Even thinking was a struggle, like straining to see through a heavy morning fog.

I watched that shiny blue-green beetle. It worked slowly, seeming to consider which way to move over the little stones and leaves in its path. I felt like that inside of myself, like I was working just to get through each moment, each day. As though if I weren't careful, I might trip and fall. To relieve the tingling in my legs, I stopped squatting and sat down. A rush of warm air from across the ravine caught my attention. Looking up I saw a woman standing in the shadow of a tree there and I had to strain to see her face. It was an odd moment, as I would normally have said, "Hello," but I didn't. When she turned toward me, the light filtering through the leaves caught in the creases of her face. She was old, very old from the look of her, and she smiled at me with a sweet, playful grin. I could see she had a long, old-fashioned skirt with a shirt hanging out that went in at the waist. Her hair was up, not hanging down, and she had a shawl over her shoulders like Mrs. Freeman sometimes wore at night when she sat in the front room.

Our eyes held, and I was caught in an unfolding of emotions; relief, peace, love, joy. Time stopped as I looked back at pictures that played through my mind— Grandpa walking out of the barn, Momma sewing in the front room, this same old woman in a chair on the porch, a baby playing on the kitchen floor. My face felt funny and I realized I was smiling. The baby was me! That's when she turned and walked back up the hill. As I watched her, she disappeared. She was gone. The fog had cleared a little from my head and for the first time in a long while, I was happy.

Even now, I can feel the ease from the endless, gripping pain I'd been living with as it released me in that moment. I sat there awhile longer, with a quiet mind and heart. The relief that came over me was a marked difference from the way I'd been, and the smile stayed put as I stood, folded my momma's birthday quilt and started up the hill to go home to Mrs. Freeman's.

I had been sick to my stomach a lot since the fire. It seemed like all I ever ate was soup and bread. Mrs. F was always baking things she hoped I would eat, but somehow everything made me think of Grandpa and then my stomach would feel queasy.

When I got back from the ravine, I considered telling Mrs. F about the lady I had seen, but I held back. It just seemed like mine to know, so I kept quiet about it.

"Hi Mary, did you have a nice walk?" she asked.

"Yes. I was watching a beetle and thinking about

how hard they work to go such a short way. I feel like that sometimes."

"What do you mean?"

"Since the fire, I'm careful, too, just like the beetle, inside myself and outside. Sometimes just walking seems hard. I feel like I have to be careful to keep going and not fall down. Does that make sense?"

"Why, yes, I think that must be exactly right. How smart you are to think of that," she said, smiling at me.

"Momma's quilt has gotten dirty. Would it be all right if we washed it?" I asked.

"I think that's a fine idea. I've been waiting for you to ask. I know you like to have it with you all the time. We'll put it in the machine and then hang it out on the line. It's a perfect day to have it dry in the breeze. Would you like to call Tommy to come over? He's been wanting to see you."

Tommy had stopped by a few times already, but I hadn't been interested in playing. His momma had dropped him off once or twice for baking day, and I had tried to be polite, but it still didn't feel right to have fun.

"I don't know. I just don't know what we would do. Everything reminds me..." I broke off and ran to my room. Overwhelmed with images of the fire, Grandpa, and playing in the lake, I hid on the closet floor. I must have dropped the quilt when I ran out of the kitchen because I was lying there shaking in the dark with the door closed and with just a bit of light coming in from under the door. I put my head down on a pair of sneakers, and the musty smell wrapped around me as I cried and cried. From under the door, I saw Mrs. F's feet. I heard a slight jiggle as she put her hand on the knob, but she must have thought better about opening the door.

"Mary," she said, "it's all going to be okay. I'm right here when you are ready to come out."

I fell asleep after that. My dreams took me back to the ravine, face to face with a different woman. I could see her clearly. She was very young and beautiful. She had Momma's face, the face from the photograph. In my dream, I knew I needed to hold very still so I could hear her. She wasn't talking very loud, but I could make out the velvety softness of her voice, and it was sweet and light to my ears, like being wrapped up in cotton candy.

She said, "Mary, sweet Mary, you watched the beetle today as it accomplished great things with small, persistent steps. So it is with you, my daughter. You have the soul of a warrior and the heart of an angel. Trust and care for yourself and be your own best friend. Watch for the blue-green beetle to guide you as you learn about these important things."

I awoke with a start. I didn't understand where I was at first. But then I saw the light from under the door and remembered that I was lying on the floor in the closet. I sat up, pushing my head into the clothes that hung above me. I cracked open the door and peered into the bedroom. Right there on the floor by the door was a plate with three cookies, a glass of milk, and my Chatty Cathy doll. Mrs. F always knew how to care for me. I slid out to the bedroom floor, put my doll on my lap, and hugged her as I nibbled on the cookies, feeling the lingering vestiges of my dream.

Like a blurry lens coming into focus, I realized that my momma had come to me in the dream. What was that she had been saying, that I must care for and trust myself, be my own best friend? I wasn't sure I understood what that meant, but I sat there and thought about it. I thought about how it was to look out for Tommy when we swam in the pond or played on the swing. Tommy was always my best friend. Well, he and Chatty Cathy.

After the fire, they had found her on the front seat of Grandpa's truck. He had picked her up in town that day. Apparently, he'd planned to give Chatty Cathy to me on my birthday. At first it was hard to hold her, but now we were best friends. I guess that's what Momma meant. I thought I would try to figure this out by myself and see how to be my own best friend. After all, I had finally seen Momma and this was what she had said, so doing it must be important. It was still confusing, mind you, but it turned out to make all the difference for me. Watching for the beetles was the best part. They were so beautiful.

I walked into the kitchen to thank Mrs. F for the cookies, and found my quilt folded neatly on my chair at the table along with Tommy, who was seated in the opposite chair waiting for me. I could tell he'd been there awhile.

"Hi Mary. I hope it's okay that I came over. My ankle is good enough for me to ride my bike now so I rode over to show you. Mrs. F said I could stay awhile to see if you want to go outside. We can sit on the porch if you want." I could tell he was nervous because he was talking really fast. Tommy was a chatterbox under normal circumstances, but at that moment, I think he was afraid I'd be mad at him. I used to be annoyed when he'd worry that way, but I was glad to see him, so I didn't mind. I was still thinking about being a best friend and what that meant, the things Momma had talked about in the dream, so I said, "Sure Tommy, let's go outside."

"I'll be out front, Mrs. F, if you're looking for me."

She smiled at me and said, "Holler if you want anything."

With that we went out to the front porch and sat on the top step. He seemed careful, hesitant even, like he didn't know what to talk about or how to act around me.

"So, what have you been doing lately?" I asked him.

"Not much. Went swimming some but there's not a lot to do without you, Mary."

"I know. I'm sorry I haven't been able to play. I bet it's been tough for you…" I went on, "…with everything that happened, and then not being able to do stuff together. We're best friends and I've been thinking about that today. We've always looked out for each other and I haven't been…"

He cut me off then, "It's okay. It was so scary that day and then after, with you being here and not seeing me. I was on crutches for so long and I was scared that you were mad at me. I'm sorry, Mary. I should never have said I would go up in the barn with you. If I hadn't said yes, it wouldn't have happened."

Tommy was looking down at the step between his feet, talking quietly. It sounded like he had tears in his eyes.

"Tommy, I don't understand all of this but I do know that you were just doing what I wanted that day. You have always been with me through everything, even if it wasn't such a good idea. It was my fault what happened, not yours. We were up in the loft because of me and my big, dumb ideas, and you were being my best friend, like always."

My shoulders started to go up and down. "Mary, it's okay, please don't cry." Tommy put his arms around me and I realized that I was sobbing. Mrs. F came out to see what was going on. Silently, she sat down by us on the steps and put her arms around us both. I think I cried for a long time, because I remember getting a headache and Tommy's shirt was damp where my face had been pressed into his shoulder.

"I've been pushing away this remembering, all of the things that happened that day...Grandpa. Oh, I miss him so much. What did I do?" The tears started again, and I had to run. Flying down the stairs, I turned onto the road like I was being chased by a demon. I had some awareness of Tommy calling for me to wait and Mrs. F telling him to let me go.

I ran blindly. Tears streamed down my face. I slipped as I veered off the road and careened through the trees going downhill. Between the tears and the running I gasped for air. I felt like I couldn't breathe. "Oh Grandpa, Grandpa, please come back."

Back in the ravine, out of my mind with grief, I was screaming at the sky and pounding the ground. The day of the fire was tumbling in on me, like a series of photographs and bursts of sound.

"Where is Grandpa? Get him out of the barn. Let me go." Then strong arms took hold of me and carried me into the house.

"Keep her here, Dorothy. I have to go and see if there's any help for Gerald." It was Tommy's dad talking to Mrs. F. My head was all blurry, and I was lashing out at Mrs. F to let me go. I tasted smoke and smelled my own panic.

She got right in my face, real close and said, "Stop, Mary. You have got to let the men help your grandpa. If you go running out there you will be in the way and that won't help him." She was loud, but quiet too, and I gave in and slumped down on the floor, staring out the screen door at the barn. I felt the fog envelope me. That's when I went away, in my mind and my heart. Now, for the first time, the fog was lifting.

Coming back to the present, I vaguely noticed that my teeth were chattering and I was holding myself. Rubbing my face I expected to feel the grit of the ashes from that day, when I suddenly felt a warmth come around me. I lifted up my eyes and saw in front of me the woman's face from my dream.

"Momma?" I said.

"Mary," she whispered as she reached out her hand to me. I reached back and my hand was drawn into hers. It felt like dipping my fingers into warm milk—I was home. I looked at her in wonder, filled with relief and held by the loving embrace of her smile. I could feel myself healing. I felt her feelings becoming mine and knew that everything would be all right.

"Mary, it's okay honey, it's all okay. There are many

things at work in life that cause other things to happen. We cannot control any of that, we can only control ourselves, and the things we choose to do. Do you understand? Forgive yourself now. Let go and notice all the good around you. You have Mrs. F, Tommy, a warm and loving home, and your special treasures. Choose to keep those things in your thoughts along with the sunshine and the happiness that come to you in so many ways every day. Choose that, Mary. Choose to notice. Choose joy."

"But, Momma, how can I when I'm the one who made the fire that killed Grandpa? And I lost all of your pretty things just when I had found them."

"You didn't lose them all. You have the most important thing that I left for you, and that's yourself. You have your birthday quilt, too, to wrap my love around you, and you have the photograph of us in the frame with the flowers to look at and feel me holding you. Those are the things I wanted you to have all along."

She went on, "Yes, you did go up to the loft with the candles, but you did not cause the wind to blow, you did not tell Grandpa to go into the barn, and you did not place the gasoline where it would cause the barn to burn so quickly. Do you see? There are many things that created the events of that day, but only a few that were in your control. Honey, forgive yourself. No one blames you, not Grandpa, not me. Now it's your turn... stop blaming yourself."

I looked down and saw the beetle again, "Mary, it's very important that you understand. Earlier you noticed how hard the beetle has to work to accomplish a small step. But that's an important step to the beetle. So it is with you in understanding this. You choose the actions you take in life and sometimes those choices lead to hurt and suffering. This happens to everyone. Now you must choose to learn the lessons, and Mary, trust yourself. I know that seems hard right now, but with each mistake you learn, and that's how you grow and make things better."

The breeze was coming down the ravine. I noticed the leaves stir around my feet. For a brief moment I was distracted by the feel of the air on my arms and face, and then I realized that I was sitting alone on those old leaves. I was okay though. I was deep in thought, pondering what Momma had said, and I felt calm. I stayed that way for some time, I think.

The light was changing as I took a stick and made patterns in the dirt around me, considering all that Momma had said. It was hard to think about the choice I had made and how it took Grandpa away. "Mistake" didn't seem like a big enough or bad enough word. But I was thinking about what Momma told me, and I guess big or little, a mistake is just that. It wasn't as hard to remember now.

The next morning Mrs. F was surprised to see me in the kitchen. "Mary, how nice to see you up bright and early this morning." Mrs. F was all smiles, same as always. This was the first morning she didn't have to get me up and she was happy to see me.

"Good morning. I've decided to go with you to milk the cows this morning."

"I welcome the company. Bessie and Bedelia will be glad to see you."

I smiled at that and sat down to eat. "Me too. I've missed them."

As we ate our bacon, eggs, and grits, Mrs. F told me about some of the changes at the farm. I think she wanted to prepare me. She said that there was a shed now, close to where the barn had been. The shed was for sheltering the cows and storing some hay and supplies. It was smaller than the barn had been. Some folks had helped to build it after the fire to keep the farm going.

It wasn't until some years later that I realized the farm kept going during that time out of the goodness of people's hearts. Truth was, after my grandpa, there wasn't anyone else left in our family besides me. He had a will saying that Mrs. F was to care for me, and that the farm was to be sold to provide for my needs.

Since I was lost in my head during those months after the fire, folks came around and take took turns helping with chores to keep things going until I could say my goodbyes properly to the farm. Mrs. F had been the one to make all of this happen. The man at the bank and my grandpa's lawyer had been in charge of the business part of things and they wanted to get the farm sold. Mrs. F kept pushing to find a renter instead. There was enough money from the apple crops and some winter crops to keep Boone on half-time and make the payments for a bit.

Mrs. F was a smart business woman, and she knew from renting out her own farmland and buildings that with rent coming in, the farm payments could still be made, with a little leftover for my care. Her goal was to keep the place available for me when I got older, so I could live there if I wanted to. Mrs. F was a visionary, and as an independent woman she believed that I should be able to grow up and live on my family farm. I sure am glad for that. And I'm even happier that she was my role model.

Our farm was only five minutes' walk down the road from Mrs. F's house. We headed out after cleaning up the breakfast dishes, and she held my hand. The air was cool and smelled of spring. I felt that nervous stomach feeling, like butterflies, and as we got closer I felt a wave of panic. Mrs. F could tell because she let go of my hand and put her arm around my shoulders, pulling me into her side. Just about then we rounded the bend and the farm came into view. The barn used to be the main thing you would see as you rounded the corner, so the fact that it wasn't there was the first thing I noticed. My breath caught in my chest and we stopped for a minute. Mrs. F didn't say anything, just kept her arm around me and gave me a minute to take it in.

The shed was bright white with red trim and it was over to the right from where the barn had been. The barn site was bare; there wasn't anything there except the tractor, which was parked where the big barn door used to be. "The men decided to leave the barn spot clear to rebuild a new one in the same place. The shed can stay right where it is as extra storage close to the new barn."

I just nodded my head that I understood, even though her words and the sight of what had changed were overwhelming. She said, "Are you ready to go on?"

"Uh-huh." I replied.

From where we stopped, the road started down a hill and then the lane into our place came up on the right. Once on the lane, the house was a ways further down, on the left-hand side. When the barn had been there, it had been located on the other side of the lane, across from the house. I could see the new shed that was now in that area and noticed that the fence had been changed for Bessie and Bedelia so they could walk in there for shelter.

We went into the shed first to get some hay and grain for the cows. It was nice inside, not big like the barn, but clean; and it smelled like new wood. Right away, I noticed that something was different. The milk storage tank wasn't there and there weren't any milking buckets.

"Where are the milking supplies?" I asked. "How are we going to milk the cows?"

"We've been giving them a rest from milking. They get to eat and graze now for the time being. I think it agrees with them. They look fat and healthy."

The sight of Bessie and Bedelia filled my heart, and being close to them felt reassuring. With an armload of hay and a bucket of grain, I walked in to the feeding area and breathed in their smell. I felt the warmth coming off of their big bodies as they pushed up around me at the feed trough, and I was immediately folded into a safe, familiar place. My stomach eased as I tossed the hay into the feed trough and sprinkled the grain on top. I savored the moment, pausing between them and listening to the munching sound as they ate their breakfast.

Putting the grain scoop back into the barrel I asked, "Can we go into the house?"

"Yes, let's do that," and Mrs. F led the way out of the shed, across the barn site to the house.

"I've left everything pretty much alone here. I wanted you to have your time looking through things."

She opened the door and stepped into the kitchen. I followed right behind her and stopped short at the faint odors of Grandpa and a lifetime of meals that lingered in the air. I missed home so much—this home. I didn't feel normal anywhere else. My room at Mrs. F's didn't feel quite right to me, and standing in the kitchen, I realized how much I wanted to be back here in my own house.

She must have noticed my reaction, "You're okay, Mary, take a couple of deep breathes." I did what she said and my head cleared. As I was breathing in, I noticed a musty smell that was stronger than it used to be. I also noticed another smell, a good smell, Momma's perfume.

"Mrs. F," I started kind of hesitantly, "do you smell that nice perfume smell?"

"No..." she said, looking at me quizzically.

"I think that is my momma's perfume smell, and I first noticed it in the days before the fire. Can I please tell you what happened?"

"Of course, Mary. Sit down here at the table. I will get you a glass of water, and you can tell me all about it."

I began to tell her all about the séances that Tommy and I had been holding in those days before the fire. The whole story just came tumbling out of me, and once I got going I couldn't have stopped if I'd wanted to. Truth was that it felt so good to tell it all to someone. She seemed to know already. The story just kept right on going through the lady in the ravine and my momma in the closet dream and then back in the ravine again. Mrs. F listened patiently. When the story had all run out, I noticed the breeze coming through the kitchen door, moving right past us sitting at the table. I put my head down on my arms on the table and stared out the door.

I asked, "What do you think of all of that, about my momma coming to help me and teach me things?"

"I think that sometimes people want something so much that they begin to see and hear things that help them feel better. I think séances and such are the work of the devil, Mary and can be very dangerous. It's good that you shared this all with me because you need to stop this now. Your momma used to go about these same kinds of things, and I worried for her soul and I told her as much. We're good Christians, Mary, and God doesn't keep with such nonsense." She sounded upset.

I felt ambushed. I did not expect this reaction and I guess I hadn't seen this side of Mrs. F before. I was embarrassed now, and mad. I knew what I'd seen and heard. I knew my momma was around me and the old lady from the ravine, too, so to heck with her.

I wanted to stand up and walk right out of there, but something caught in my head. What was that she'd said about Momma being the same way? So I asked her what she'd meant.

"That's right Mary, Celia used to go to the ravine too. You know, your lives are very similar in that your grandma, her momma, also died when Celia was quite young. She, too, wondered about many things, just as you have. You know, she and my Maddie were best friends, and Celia would always be over to our house. She had periods of time when she was questioning why she was without her momma and then questions about growing up. She and I were close, and I loved her so. I gave her the guidance I could, and I told her it was just her imagination when she talked about seeing ghosts and that she should forget such things."

Then I asked her, "Did she see an old woman, too, like I did?"

"Stop it now, Mary."

"Did she?"

"I don't see how it makes any difference, but your momma thought she saw your Great Great Grandma Gert. Gert was quite a character and beloved in your family. Celia had grown up hearing stories about her, and I knew she was just making up things about hearing and seeing Gert. You must have heard your grandpa mention her. Well, I told Celia that's all it was, just imaginings and such. Imagination is one thing, and that I can abide, but there are not ghosts or séances and such, so you best be letting that go now. Do you understand Mary? God has His laws and those things are the work of the devil."

Ha. Grandpa had never put much store in God and

going to church. We hadn't always gone on Sundays, and we never talked about it around home. Great Great Grandma Gert must be the other woman I'd seen in the ravine that first day. Mrs. F could go on all she wanted about the devil, but now I knew what I needed to know. Having Momma around was the best thing that had ever happened to me and could not possibly be the devil's work.

I'd gotten what I wanted, and I wasn't inclined to show my mad feelings, so I got up and began to wander through the house. As I walked into the sitting room, the sight of Grandpa's chair set me stumbling backward. I froze in place. My eyes welled up, and I felt entirely alone. Last time I had been in here was the day of the fire. I put my hands over my ears as the sounds of that day filled my head and I heard a scream I had not recalled before. My grandpa's scream—that horrible and awful sound tore through me and I fell to the floor.

Chapter Three

I woke up lying on the bed in my room upstairs. Slowly, I focused on the familiar sight of the curtain floating over my face with the breeze coming through the window. My eyes wandered around the room. I hadn't been here for a long time and it was comforting to see familiar things. I wanted so much to be living here again.

I thought of the time when I had fallen asleep with all of those pictures around me on my rug on the floor. I got up and went over to the dresser and opened the drawer where I'd put my shoebox of pictures. It was still there. My clothes were all gone—I knew they were in my room at Mrs. F's—but the pictures were still in my drawer where I'd left them. Just then, I heard voices coming from downstairs in the kitchen. I thought I heard Boone and Mrs. F talking. I realized he must have helped get me upstairs because last I remembered I had been in the sitting room. *Oh no...Grandpa's chair...the scream.* I took a few breaths, and with each breath I felt a little quieter inside. Then I thought about the beetle and how this was a big hard step and how I had to be persistent. That was a big word for me, but Grandpa used to say it and I knew it meant to stick to something. I knew I had to stick to taking care of myself and get past this hard time.

I clutched my box of pictures and stood up from the rug. I closed the dresser drawer and walked out to the hall. I knew that squeaky top stair would let them know I was awake and coming downstairs. Boone and Mrs. F were sitting there at the table and looked up when I walked in.

I stopped in the doorway to the kitchen.

"How are you feeling Mary?" Mrs. F asked, looking at me from across the table.

"I guess I'm okay," I wasn't feeling much like talking to her.

"You've had a big morning. Do you want to go back to the house? We can come back again soon."

"I don't see why I can't just live here. I can take care of myself. This is my home."

She looked at me and seemed stunned, "You can't take care of yourself in this big house. But you can come back here to live someday...when you're older. Besides, we need to get a renter in the place."

That was all I could take. She didn't think I could take care of myself, and she was going to let someone else live in Grandpa's and my house. I couldn't hear any more of that and I took off out the door towards the pond.

As I ran down the hill, the breeze blew my bangs into my face. They had gotten long, and I was brushing them out of my eyes as I came upon the bench. I was practically on top of it when I realized someone was there. It was the old lady from the ravine. I was startled and let out a little sound that had her to turning around. I had never seen a face like that before, old and wrinkled, but soft and sweet too. Her eyes were a startling shade of blue-green, deeply kind and twinkly with laughter. Looking at her made me smile, and I felt like I knew her, like I'd always known her. As I stood there smiling, she said, "Hi, Honey, I'm your Great Great Grandma Gert, happy to make your acquaintance. Would you like to join me?"

It took me a minute, but I smiled right back at her. I felt like laughing because meeting her felt so good. That's how it felt all around her, good and joyful.

I said, "Yes, I'm so excited to meet you too."

Her focus was on my box of pictures, which was still clutched to my chest.

"It's been awhile since you were here," she said.

I was looking more closely at Grandma Gert now. She had on the same long skirt and shirt that hung out over it, just like she'd been wearing when I first saw her. She wore a wide brown leather belt that wrapped around her waist. The belt was old and worn. I'd seen that belt before, but I wasn't sure where.

"I've always felt good here at the pond. It's my special place, mine and Tommy's. This is my farm, and I should get to live here. I mean, I know that it's my fault that I can't..." and my voice trailed off then.

"I know what you mean. I always feel good here at the pond, too," said Gert. "Did your momma talk to you about the beetle?"

"How did you know about that? Were you in the ravine yesterday when I was there? I think I saw you."

She smiled. "The beetle works so hard to take a small yet mighty step. You have done that in this last day. I used to teach your momma many things, when she was about your age. Your momma was a sweet and loving girl, just like you. She had a load of pain that she carried with her."

"I feel that way sometimes," I said, happy to hear a way that I was the same as my momma, "even before the fire..."

"Let me tell you a story. I was feisty like you when I was a girl. Never did listen to my pa. My ma was patient with me, even when I'd run off and rip my dress doing something I wasn't s'posed to do. Without saying a word, she'd set me down and teach me how to mend my own clothes. When I didn't come in with the water after she sent me to the crick, she'd have to come on herself and find me. There I'd be, messing with some critter or another. Ma would have me fill my bucket and walk back with her and the bucket. I'd carry it back, as if I was still doing the chore on my own. I learned patience being with Ma, and as the years went by that meant being patient with myself. Patient and persistent...like the beetle."

I was staring at her eyes. That's where I had seen

that bright blue-green color of her eyes before, the bee-tle.

"How can I be patient when what I did was so bad? You know my grandpa is gone because I didn't do what I was told. There's no forgiving that."

"You have been looking for your ma, and now you've found her. Bad things happen, make no mistake, and this was a bad one for sure. Thing is, if you pay close attention and give it some time, you'll see something good always comes out of something not so good."

I was staring at her now. Watching her face move with all those lines and wrinkles was fascinating. Her skin was paper thin and it was something to look at.

She went on, "I loved riding my horse fast when I was a girl. Festus was his name. I had him 'til I turned 16. One day, Festus and I went out to run along the road that went into town. Ma sent me on some errand or other to the neighbor's, and I couldn't have been happier." Gert smiled at the recollection.

"I got him saddled and off we went. Soon as I was out of sight of the house, I took off running down that road, even though I surely did know better. Going fast was in our blood, Festus and me. That wind in my face felt like freedom. As we rounded the last corner before the neighbors, just as I was about to slow him down, there was a wagon broken down in the middle of the road. I pulled the reigns to the left, and Festus and I tumbled head over heels. Off the side of the road and down the hill we toppled. I was thrown clear when we rolled into the trees, and I heard the crack of his back when he banged into one of them."

She paused then, and I was hanging onto her every word, waiting for her to go on.

"Before this happened I was more than sure that I could handle anything that came my way. After that day, it took a while for me to believe that again. But eventually I did."

"How? How did you come to believe again?"

"At first, I was mighty tough on myself, like you've been. My ma was always the one who'd taught me, and I told you how patient she was. Well, she listened and let me cry it out for some time after that. Then, when my crying all seemed to be done, she told me this, 'Gert, weren't no other way to learn this lesson about living. Sometimes we've got to lose something precious to us in order to learn how to take care of ourselves. The pain after such a thing can be mighty overwhelming, but it's sticking with the work of growing that will get you through.'"

My stomach was growling, and I heard Mrs. F calling for me. "I'm so sorry that you lost Festus. I think I know how you felt."

"I think you do too."

"I better go now. I don't want Mrs. F to come down here and see you. Would she be able to see you?"

"No, Dorothy wouldn't be able to see me. You go on and we will be together another time soon. Remember what we talked about. Now give me a hug, girl."

Not having hugged a ghost before, I hesitated for a moment. Then, I put my arms around her and I felt whole. It was comfort, pure and simple. This was my great great grandma, and she was helping me find my way home.

"Go on now, Mrs. F has a pot of your favorite chicken noodle soup on for dinner."

I turned to go and then turned right back around to wave at her, but she was already gone. With a little smile on my face, I shook my head in wonder.

When I got up to the house, Mrs. F was glad to see me.

"It's been a while since I've seen a smile on your face, and it sure looks good. How are you feeling?"

"I feel happy." My mad was all gone. I smiled up at her, and we started our walk home.

Chapter Four

The next day I woke up thinking about Gert and how I wanted to know more about her. When I get an idea, I tend to hang on to it until I work it out. I thought I would go with Mrs. F to the farm and get up into the attic. Since she wanted me to go through the things in the house, it might be easy to get her permission to go there. I was fixed on finding the old albums and hoping with all I was worth to find a picture of Gert. I was going to be careful with how I brought this up with Mrs. F though. No more sharing my special stories. But since she was the only person that could give me any more information about my great great grandma and Momma, I would have to figure out a way to bring this subject up safely, without her talking about the devil. I hoped it would be easy if I could find the albums.

Ready then to get up, my feet were all tangled in the

covers as another thought came to me. *Maddie... Sure, that was it. Being Momma's best friend, I'm sure she could tell me some stories. But she wasn't coming until the summer and that was too long to wait.*

Mrs. F was in the kitchen when I got there.

"I'd like to go along with you again this morning to the farm."

"Really? Well good then. I've some dusting to do in the house and I could use a hand."

As we walked along I said, "I've been thinking about some old albums that Grandpa had up in the attic. I'd like to go up there today and look for them."

"That's a fine idea. I haven't gotten up there yet to go through things so how about we go together?" Mrs. F said.

This is going to work, I thought.

She went on, "We've got a little extra time this morning. Let's do it right after we take care of the barn chores."

Distracted with my wonderings about Gert, I hurried to get the cows fed. When we got to the house I was first inside, smiling to myself as I inhaled my momma's lovely smell. I kept that to myself.

We went up the stairs out of the kitchen to the bedroom hall and pulled down the attic ladder. It creaked as it unfolded. I never was too keen on going up to the attic before, but this was exciting. I felt the rush of cool air as the steps came down with the door. Being early in the day, it was chilly up there. I pulled my sweater around me. Mrs. F went first and reached for the pull string to turn on the ceiling light. It felt so still and quiet.

"Do you remember where you saw the photo books?" she asked.

"I think they were in some boxes over in the back corner, behind that screen."

"That sure is an old dressing screen. Must be from your great great grandma's time."

"You mean Grandma Gert?" I asked.

"Yes, sometime around then."

Perfect, I thought.

"Mrs. F, will you please tell me about Great Great Grandma Gert? I don't know much about her.

She looked at me for a minute, and then said, "I knew her. She passed on when your Momma Celia was a little girl. It was bittersweet. She went on in her sleep, sitting in her rocker on the front porch of this house. She lived here with your momma's family. She outlasted all of her children and some of her grandchildren. Of course her husband too. I think his name was Harvey."

"My Ben and I moved in down the road...oh, I guess it was 1930, and I was expecting Maddie." Mrs. F sat down on a stack of suitcases as she talked and she was staring off, smiling and remembering.

"Your grandma and grandpa were neighborly folks. Your grandma brought us one of her wonderful apple pies, and your Grandpa Gerald came around too, offering Ben any help he needed getting our farm up and going. It was a good feeling to have such friendly folks right down the road, and we all became friends. Your

Grandma Rita and I had our babies about the same time, later that first year. Gert was a big help to both of us. She was always a help with everything. It seemed there wasn't anything she couldn't do, including mending a fence or bringing fish in for supper. Gert was something special with those unusual blue-green, laughing eyes. It felt good to be around her. No matter what help a person needed, Gert would put them at ease and step right in to get things done. She was very wise."

I stared at Mrs. F, glued to her every word. It struck me then how Grandpa used to say things about "Ma" but not very often, most likely because he didn't talk about much of anything very often, except maybe the weather and the farm.

"Grandpa used to say things about Ma sometimes Mrs. F. Who was that?"

"That would have been Gert he was talking about. That's what he called her, "Ma." Even though she was actually his wife's grandma, everybody called her Ma."

This felt really important to me. It was as if my world just got a lot wider, or maybe deeper. I was beginning to have a sense of my roots. The kind that come from knowing about the people who came before me, the ones whose lives helped to form and create the beginnings of who I was and where I came from.

Whether I knew the people who came before me or not, I could see that their lives wrote part of my life. For me, it was this farm, my grandpa, and Mrs. F that were here for me even before I was born. I could see that my life was just another square on a quilt, that life is like that, a big endless patchwork of people and choices and feelings. Patches that we add to the ever-growing patchwork of our families. This was a really big thought and it felt good, like I belonged.

Mrs. F got up then and went looking for the album. Behind the screen in a corner by the window, we found the box. There wasn't a cover on it or flaps, so the albums were dusty, sitting right on top. I reached in and lifted out the first one. As I opened the cover, an old photograph fell out onto the floor. I stooped down to pick it up and saw that there were several people in the picture. Mrs. F said, "Why, there she is, right there in the chair. That's your Great Great Grandma Gert. Standing over to her right is your Grandma Rita and there's Grandpa Gerald. Do you recognize him?"

That was hard. He looked so young. I did see some of my grandpa in that face looking out from the photograph. "Yes, I do recognize him. Who are the people on the other side?"

"That would be your great grandma and grandpa. Three generations of your folks Mary, with your momma on the way. See your Grandma Rita? By the looks of her she was expecting your momma. This must have been taken about the time we moved here."

I looked at Mrs. F and I felt a lot of appreciation for having her to tell me all of this.

"Thank you for taking care of me and for sharing these stories too. I know sometimes I can be difficult, but I'm lucky to have you."

She stopped and reached over to draw me in for a hug. Pressed into her chest, smelling of fresh bread and soap, I leaned in to the warmth of her arms around me. Hugs had been rare for me over the years. Come to think of it, Mrs. F was about the only person who'd ever hugged me. She and Maddie, that is, when she was around. Something shifted in my heart. There was a little stir in the air that I barely felt on my arms. Peaking over Mrs. F's shoulder I noticed a bright light all around us. Momma and Gert were smiling and holdings hands, in the corner by the screen. Poor Mrs. F, she was missing all the fun. I smiled back, feeling safe and tender as I held on to that moment. It was the best moment ever.

Chapter Five

A few months went by and Dorothy said I was grow-ing right before her eyes. I had a healthy appetite again and she said, "It's good to see you making up for lost time. You're growing like a weed." I started calling her Dorothy after our morning in the attic. She thought Mrs. F was too formal and I think we both felt closer that way.

Tommy's ankle improved, but it was never as good again as it had been before the fire. Several bones had broken and never mended properly because his ankle hadn't been set right. Our community was more re-mote then and there was one doctor in the area. No one thought to take Tommy to the hospital in the next county over. Since broken bones weren't usually consid-ered a big deal, they assumed that Doc could take care of him just fine.

After Dorothy and I found the photo albums, I was anxious to tell Tommy everything that had happened with Gert and Momma.

"I just don't know, Mary," he said. "After the séances and all that happened, I think you should leave all of this alone. I wish you wouldn't talk about it anymore. It gives me the creeps."

That felt really bad and I was embarrassed.

"You're wrong," I said, feeling my cheeks get hot. "I'm sorry I told you anything."

Trembling as I kept myself from crying, I got up then to go home, feeling indignant and more alone than ever.

We had to get over our upset pretty quick, since we were best friends and counted on each other for company. But I found myself holding back after that. Whenever I had a visit with Momma or Gert I wanted to tell him about it, but I didn't.

Late March I started back to school part time. I was behind, but the teacher went easy on me. I'd always been an able student and I worked at home with Dorothy too, so I did okay. I made do anyway. Overhearing the kids at school, I knew that there were stories going around about our barn burning down; that I was some kind of witch or something and had started the fire. Ha! Where did they get that? Witches had brooms and cast spells. I was just doing séances to talk to Momma. That's all it was. But I guess that people think differently about all that, like Tommy and Mrs. F. So I came to accept that people thought I was different. And I guess I was. It was lonely believing in things that no one else understood and even more so now that Tommy didn't believe me either. I'd always been able to share everything with him, and that was hard.

I had gone back to school after Easter and I kept spending time in the ravine and at the pond, visiting Momma and Gert. I felt a comfort that I had never known before, and that was the gift that came out of an otherwise awful experience. I missed my grandpa. I still had bouts of blaming myself and occasional nightmares about the fire. I would wake up and think about what Momma had said, that I can only control me and the things that I do and that there are many things beyond my control. Gert was teaching me too and some days it wasn't so easy to understand the lessons, but I kept at it.

"Values," she would say. "That's the thing to have and to live by."

"What do you mean, values?"

"Well, say you're helping Dorothy with baking. That's being helpful, and that's a value...same as doing your chores."

"Doing my schoolwork, too?"

"Now, that's being responsible, and that's a value too."

"It's important to think about what your values are and to live each day true to those values. That's living from your heart, and that makes a happy life."

"I can do that," I said.

"Of course you can, as you already do and you will keep on. It takes practice, though. Sometimes you might get off track with other things. Just keep an eye on yourself and observe Mary. When you don't feel so good about something, you might be forgetting your values."

With confusion swirling through my head, I decided to let it go then. I knew how wise Gert was and that with time I'd get it figured out, even if it was a little hard to understand right then.

Maddie came for a visit early in the summer. The days were longer and the buzz of the crickets kept me out playing past supper. She brought her two children, who were a little older than I. Mark was thirteen and Emmy was already eleven. They lived in the city, Springfield. I couldn't imagine the city. I'd never been to one. The day they arrived I felt shy. I had always known them from their visits while I was at home with Grandpa but we never got real close. Being down the road, I didn't see them much and they never came to play when I invited them to the pond. They usually left me out of stuff and I figured they thought I wasn't as good or as smart as they were.

"They're here." Dorothy ran out the door and I came along behind her. With big hugs and a smile, she held on tight to Mark and Emmy.

Maddie got out of the car and came around to give me a hug, "Hi, honey," she smiled as she walked up to me, "it's so good to see you." Maddie was nice to me. It felt comforting when she hugged me, and I felt important too. As though her kids might like me better.

"Mark, Emmy, say hi to Mary."

They shuffled over to me and stopped a little short, "Hello."

I tried to smile, "Hi."

Dorothy hustled us all into the house since it was almost suppertime. She had done it up big with ham, corn on the cob, her fresh rolls, and a bean salad. Then there were brownies for dessert. This was one of the good things about having them come for a visit. Dorothy cooked up more of her special dishes with company around.

After supper we all went upstairs to settle them into their bedrooms. There were three bedrooms in the house, and before I came along, Maddie used her old room when she visited and Mark and Emmy used the guest room. Maddie's old room was my room now, so she bunked with me.

Plopping her bag on the bed, she started to unpack.

"I'm so glad you have this room. I loved growing up here and you will too. I can still hear your momma and me giggling and sharing secrets, snuggled up on that front window seat. The morning sun would stream in those windows and then by afternoon be shining in the other side of the room through that dormer. Yes, it's a good place to dream and imagine."

I did really like that room when I let myself think about it. I still wanted my own room back, but I was starting to feel cozy there. I had discovered the calm of nestling into those window seats and looking out both sides of the house, off into the distance. With big oak trees right outside the windows, I watched squirrels playing and the farmer who came and worked Dorothy's farm too. It was a good place to imagine, and to go through my picture box.

I had two twin beds, so it worked out well for Maddie and me to share the room. This was especially great because at night I could talk to Maddie alone. The first night, when we were going to sleep, I asked her about Momma. I felt a little shy doing this, but wanting to know about Momma was always in me.

"Oh Mary, I miss your momma still. She and I were always together growing up. We were so close in age and lived right down the road from each other. The pond on your farm was our favorite place to play, so we would be there a lot of the summer, just like you and Tommy. In fact, we were each other's best friends all of our lives. When I left for Springfield to go to secretarial school your momma and I cried buckets the whole week before. I mean I was excited, but leaving Celia was harder even than leaving my own momma and daddy. Celia and I were always different in that I wanted to move away from the farm life, and the farm was in her blood. All she ever wanted was to get married, have a family, and live on her family farm forever, just like Grandma Gert."

"I know about Great Great Grandma Gert. I have a picture of her with my other grandparents, and Dorothy told me all about how special she was." I was careful not to say about how Gert came and visited me.

"Grandma Gert was a family legend. Sometimes I would listen to Celia talk about her and wonder how she knew so many of the stories. There was this one about how Grandma Gert had taken a fall on her horse as a teenager and the horse had died. When Celia told me that one I remember thinking that it sounded like she had heard it firsthand."

"You know, I sometimes thought your momma had special powers when we were girls. That may sound crazy, but there was something about how she told those stories. Then there were the times she would get a premonition about something that was about to happen, and it did."

I looked at Maddie, trying to figure out what she knew. I did not want to fall into a trap by telling her too much, but I was itching to tell Maddie about the ravine and Gert visiting me. Even how I'd talked to Momma. I didn't know what to do.

"I'm getting pretty sleepy Mary. We can talk more about this tomorrow, okay?"

"Maddie, do you think Momma could see Grandma Gert?"

Well, there it was. I let it out alright.

"What do you mean, see her?"

"Dorothy told me once that my momma would go to the ravine and talked about how Grandma Gert would visit with her there. Your momma got pretty mad about that too. Said it was the devil's work and all. Did you know about that?"

"She talked to you about this? That surprises me. Ma would get really upset about all Celia's stories. It goes against church teachings and she worried for Celia. I did too, but I also got to hear Celia tell me about these visits in the ravine so I was never quite sure what I thought. Even now, I can't say as I'm really sure. Celia's stories were so convincing, and like I said, she knew so much about Grandma Gert that I don't think she could have known otherwise. I would always leave it alone since I never really knew. What ended up being important to me is that it helped your momma. Why did Ma tell you about this?"

"Because I see Gert. And Maddie, I see Momma too."

She sat up in bed then. "What? You see Celia?"

"Yeah, I see them both. I first smelled Momma's perfume when I was doing a séance with Tommy one day in the old barn." There, I'd done it again; it was all spilling out now.

She said, "Séance Mary? Tell me everything now." And I did. I told her the whole awful story about the fire. When I was done, I was kind of scared that she would tell me it was all the devil's work, but I waited to see what she would say.

"I wasn't really sure how all that happened. I heard some things about it from Ma, but I'm glad to hear it all from you. I'd say you're even more like your momma than I ever knew. You look like her, that's plain to see, but you think like her too. Mary, I'm so sorry that happened. You must have been feeling so responsible for your grandpa. Tell me about that."

"It's been really hard. Momma and Gert have helped me a lot. But I can tell by how people are around me that folks think I'm odd. I was never real popular. I've felt different for about as long as I can remember. But I only started to understand that last summer when I was doing the séances and missing Momma so much. It felt like if I could find her maybe I wouldn't feel so different, you know? So that's how it all started, and what an awful idea that turned out to be. It's my fault what happened to grandpa."

"Mary, that's nonsense. You mustn't think such a thing. It was an accident plain and simple. They happen all the time to all sorts of folks. There was a lot that went on that day that you couldn't have known would happen, and if just one of those things had been different, there never would have been a fire. Bad things happen, Mary, and we go on. Somewhere along the way, if we watch real close, we will see the good that comes out of it. I know that sounds crazy and all, but it's true. From every hard thing comes something else that we need to know, to learn.

"That's what Momma said, Maddie. Just about the same way she said it too."

Maddies' eyes were wide as she looked at me. "This is almost too much for me, Mary. To think of Celia actually communicating with you," she stopped there as her voice got hoarse and she couldn't speak real plain. Then I saw she was crying.

"Why are you crying?'

"I miss her so. I want to see her too. I guess I'm not surprised that you see her. I also think this settles the question of her seeing Grandma Gert as a girl. It must be so."

I said, "I know that Dorothy can't see them because when I was at the pond one day with Gert, she told me Dorothy can't see her."

"Well that makes sense, or I would have been able to see her all those years ago with Celia. I think I need to sleep on all of this."

Reaching out toward me, I went to Maddie for a hug. " I'm glad you told me everything."

"Me too. I'm so happy to get to talk about it with someone. I feel a lot better." I was smiling as I lay my head down. The moon was shining across my bed, and I felt peaceful as I drifted off to sleep.

The rest of the visit seemed to fly by, and it turned out to be more fun than I had expected. I was relieved after our talk that first night and I felt a new bond with Maddie. Having her love and feeling her understanding was reassuring to me. It lifted me up. It was like having Momma around to give me a real hug.

Chapter Six

Dorothy prevailed with Grandpa's banker and his lawyer, and the farm was rented to a family that summer. Mason was their name. They were nice enough and their older boy Calvin seemed like he could be a friend to Tommy and me. He was a year older but we were all going to be in the same class since he'd been held back a year. I told Tommy that we should be neighborly and go over and introduce ourselves to him, and he agreed. It was challenging for me, knowing people would be in my house, and it grabbed in my stomach to think I wouldn't be free to go to the pond whenever I wanted. I'd been working on being okay with all this, but it was hard work all the same.

So with a little apprehension that first day after the moving van arrived, we walked over with Dorothy to welcome them. We brought cinnamon rolls, a pie, and cookies to help them feel at home. It seemed strange walking up to the door at my own house and knocking. Like I said, I'd been working on preparing for this and one of the ways I'd done that was talking it through with Dorothy. For several weeks, we had gone through the house to get it ready for the new folks, and I had struggled with being mad and then accepting, and then feeling mad again. We were leaving the furniture there because they needed it. I felt especially funny about someone living in my room. I mean, it was mine.

The day I packed my few last things from my dresser and closet, I decided to carve my initials in everything. I had my pocketknife that my grandpa had given me. I knew that wouldn't be a very popular idea with Dorothy, but it was my room and she didn't need to know. So I did the carving in places that wouldn't show—the bed around on the side by the wall, the dresser inside my bottom drawer, and the closet, down on the floorboard to the right when you open the door. I carved then small, but it still took me a little while.

"What's taking so long up there?"

"I'm making everything 'just so' for the new folks," I said.

She was always giving me extra time, so it worked out okay and I felt better when I'd finished marking things as my own.

I went downstairs and found Dorothy sweeping off the porch one last time. I knew I was lucky to have Dorothy and her house to be my home, but not living at the farm, well, I never really could let that go. I guessed at that point, I was as prepared as I was ever going to be.

We knocked on the screen door, and several little

kids came running to see who was there. Right behind them was Mrs. Mason. "Oh, hello, please come in."

Dorothy hadn't met Mrs. Mason yet, since the lawyer had done all of the business about renting the place. She put out her hand and introduced herself.

"Thank you so much. My name is Dorothy Freeman. This is Tommy. He lives across the pond, and this is my girl, Mary." That helped—she said I was her girl.

"Please call me Jean, Dorothy. These here are my little ones. Megan, she's two; Chip who's five; Rex, he's seven; and my boy Calvin is coming in the door. He's just had his twelfth birthday."

"Well," said Dorothy, "it's so nice to meet you all." She turned to Calvin as he walked in the door, extended her hand to shake his, and he stepped right up to shake her hand too.

"Nice to meet you, ma'am," he smiled at her.

"It's so nice to meet you, Calvin," said Dorothy. "This is Tommy and this is my girl Mary. They have been looking forward to having you move here, especially since you all will be going to school together."

I jumped right in and shot my hand out too. He looked at me kind of funny and took my hand for a handshake.

"Hi," he said.

"Hi Calvin," I said. "I used to live on this farm, and Tommy and I know all of the good places to play and things to do. We're going to show you everything."

"I was noticing the rope swing at the pond..."

"We've been using that swing all our lives. Do you want to go down there now?" He looked at his momma, but she wasn't looking back.

"My goodness, you've brought such nice baked goods," said Mrs. Mason, as she admired the perfect pie crust Dorothy made. She went on, "You are so kind. I can clear the table here and we'll sit and have coffee and get acquainted."

"Please don't bother about that. Thank you so much for offering, but we just wanted to bring these things by and say hello and welcome you. It's nice to meet you and the children. We live back down the road, first house on the right. I've put my phone number on the paper there on top of the brownie pan. Please call if there's anything at all we can do to help."

"I will be sure to do that. I think I've got my work cut out for me getting settled here. My husband, Jeb, said that there'll be a new barn going up soon and I will have a lot of cooking to do for the men. Maybe you would think about coming over for that? I'm sure I'll need a hand, what with watching the kids and all."

"Well, of course, I'd be happy to. Mary is good help, too, in the kitchen and with the little ones. You let me know when and we'll be here."

"Thank you, Dorothy. That will be just fine. I surely will let you know."

Just then, Mr. Mason came through the door. I felt a change in the room and the kids got antsy. Mrs. Mason started talking faster.

"Jeb, this here's Dorothy Freeman from down the road. Look at all these nice things she brought to welcome us."

He glanced at us, paused and said, "Hello."

His voice sounded gravelly. "Jean, get me the checkbook, I'm goin' to town for supplies."

"Of course, it's just here in the drawer." She handed it to him, and back out the door he went, with the screen slamming behind him.

Mrs. Mason turned to me, "I'm sorry, kids, but Calvin is busy with chores. Another time soon, you two can come over, okay?"

"Sure," I said, feeling a little confused by Mr. Mason. He wasn't friendly.

We stepped outside then, onto the porch as he was getting in to his truck. He yelled over his shoulder, "Boy, you done the chores I gave you yet?" He sounded rough and it scared me.

Dorothy said, "We'll just be going now, welcome to the farm."

On the way back to Dorothy's—I guess it was really my home now—Dorothy was acting upbeat like always and saying positive things about the Masons.

"Mrs. Mason keeps a nice home. That kitchen is already looking real settled and those children seem good as gold. Calvin was very polite stepping up to shake hands and speak right out. He seems like a good boy."

"Yeah, he seemed like a good kid," said Tommy.

I kept quiet. When we shook hands it felt bad in my stomach. And his pa, well I wasn't comfortable around him either. But instead of sharing anything that could get me a funny look from Dorothy, I said, "Yes, they seem nice. I hope we can keep playing at the pond."

"We can, Mary. You heard Mrs. Mason. She said we could go over real soon."

I let it go at that.

Chapter Seven

When the time for the barn raising came along, only a week or so had passed. Tommy and I had gone over to play with Calvin one time, but his mother didn't know where he was.

So I thought, "Why not ask?"

"Would it be alright for us to go and play at the pond?"

She said yes.

"Keep an eye out for Calvin. He's around here somewhere, and I'm sure he'd like to join you."

It was one of those still, stifling hot days, and going for a swim would be just the thing to take care of that.

We headed down the hill and called for Calvin as we went along. There wasn't any sign of him, so Tommy and I decided to go for it. That swing was looking really good.

I went into the trees to put on the swimsuit that I had brought with me. Tommy pulled off his shirt and started running for the swing.

"Hey, Tommy, wait for me!"

"I'm just gonna make sure the swing is all set to go," he said with that funny little smile he had when he was joking around with me. "Hurry up and get your swimming suit on," he hollered as he ran off.

I went in the bushes just uphill from the pond, the same place I had used for changing all my life. But this time, something didn't feel right. I looked around before I changed. I couldn't shake that feeling, like someone was there watching. I hurried up to join Tommy.

I left my things on the bench where I had sat with Gert, and ran to the swing. Tommy was already in the water. I heard the splash of him landing just as I turned from the bench.

"Tommy, why didn't you wait for me? I'm gonna get you now." With that, I grabbed the rope, backed up the hill, and ran for the water line as quick as rabbit. I swung out over the water and nearly dropped on Tommy's head. I loved doing that.

"You are a crazy girl," he laughed. We splashed and played and swam for quite awhile that afternoon. When we were tired, we got out and laid on the grass by the edge of the pond, drying off in the sun.

I got quiet and said, "Tommy, when I was changing my clothes before, something didn't feel right."

"What do you mean?"

"I was in the bushes getting ready to put my swimsuit on like I have a million times before when this prickly feeling started on my skin, like someone was watching me."

"Oh you're imaging things. Everything's just the same as it's always been around here."

I felt mad and I sat right up and said, "Maybe it feels the same to you, Tommy, but not to me. You don't know what it's like to lose your only family and to have to give up your farm and your own room and everything."

With each word my anger swelled. I was sick of having to keep so much inside. I was doing my best to accept everything that had changed. I was tired of trying to sort things out going back and forth about what I could say and what I couldn't say and not being able to share about it all. It was crowded inside of me, and that day it came spewing out at Tommy.

He was sitting up now too, "Mary, I'm sorry. I don't know how it is for you and I'm real sorry. This is probably bad, but I forget about it sometimes. It seems like going on is all there is to do, but that must sound dumb to you." He looked stricken to have me so upset.

"Well, surely you can see I've done my share of that," I felt indignant. "I'm living with Dorothy and helping out. I'm trying not to be a bother, and I don't tell you the most important things I think about because you don't believe me anymore. I've even lost you as my real best friend. But you're my only friend, so I just make do with what there is."

He slowly said, "What are you talking about?"

"You stopped me from being able to share with you about Momma and Gert, so now I'm afraid to tell you a lot of stuff." That was kind of an exaggeration, but it still felt good to say. "Like how I got a bad feeling about Calvin the other day when we met him. He looked at me kind of funny, but I didn't think I could tell you that because you wouldn't believe me. Now you're telling me I'm imagining things again today. That's what I mean."

"I'm so sorry," his voice was elevated. "I don't want you to feel that way. I know you've been through a lot and more than I can understand, but I still want to be your best friend. We've always been best friends. I'm sorry I made you feel bad."

"We never have talked about the fire again and Grandpa. You were hurt so bad, and it was all my fault."

I felt the tears coming now.

"We did it together, remember? I should have been able to put the fire out."

My heart twisted, "No, you couldn't have, it happened so fast. There wasn't anything we could do but save ourselves."

I'm sorry about your grandpa. I miss him too. I'm sorry about your momma's trunk and that you can't live at home anymore. You're right, I don't have any idea how it must be for you. But you are my best friend and you always will be."

Relief flooded through me as Tommy put his hand on my knee. Feeling understood released me.

"I think you're right, I don't know. Maybe today I'm just feeling funny because other people are living here and this is the first time we've played at the pond since the Masons moved in. Maybe I was imagining things."

"Let's go on back to Mrs. F's. I'm hungry and dinner must be on by now. That will make you feel better."

My stomach was growling. "That sounds good, I'm hungry too."

"Put your clothes on over your swimsuit so we can hurry up. Your suit looks dry."

There was a slight rustling in the bushes, and I figured it was the breeze.

"Good idea. They're over on the bench."

As I put my shorts and shirt on, I noticed Tommy looking around. I was glad he was there.

Dorothy had ham sandwiches and potato chips ready for us, and a tall glass of ice-cold milk too. The smell of chocolate chip cookies baking enveloped us as we launched into eating dinner and telling her all about swimming that morning.

"Mrs. Mason called this morning while you two were gone to report that the barn will be going up in a few days."

She already knew about this, because she knew all of the farm business. Since she was my guardian, Grandpa's lawyer included her in all the farm business decisions. The materials for building the barn would be paid for by my grandpa's estate. But no one knew that Dorothy was a part of all of that. It seemed to work best that way.

"We will be going over to help on Saturday. Tommy, would you like to come too? The more the merrier," she smiled.

"I will ask my ma," Tommy said. "I think Pa will be coming to help, so I'm sure it will be alright."

I was glad to hear that.

"Good. Mary, I told Mrs. Mason that we would be

bringing pies and cookies. I've already started the cookies, and yes, you two can have some for dessert after you eat your dinner." She was smiling.

I woke up early Saturday morning and it promised to be another hot day. August was like that. We were out the door with two big baskets full of things to eat by 6:30 a.m. We knew the men would be about ready to get started, and Dorothy wanted to offer them rolls and coffee before the work got underway. We loaded the old pickup and headed down the road.

The dust was kicking up when we pulled in, with trucks and men arriving too. Our coffee and rolls were greeted with smiles of appreciation as we handed them out from the tailgate. Mrs. Mason was setting up some tables in front of the house, and Mr. Mason was showing the men around, talking about what was going where and giving out assignments. There were big piles of lumber and other things for building the barn. More trucks were pulling in with neighbor fellas, and Tommy and his pa were among them. Tommy hopped out and said he was going to help haul lumber. I handed him a roll and he winked.

Energy was high with all the neighbors there to help. The morning was moving right along and the screen door kept banging as we went in and out of the kitchen, preparing food and setting up for noon dinner. Heavy air was filled with sounds of saws and shouts, and the shape of my new barn was coming up from the dirt. The tables were piled high to keep hungry men fueled for work. For a fleeting moment, I thought of how much had changed in the last year and suddenly tears for Grandpa pricked my eyes. It took a moment to blink them away.

I was keeping an eye on little Megan. Being only two years old, this was a dangerous situation for her. She seemed so vulnerable with her small frame and curly blond pigtails. We had taken to each other immediately, and I looked down to find her close by, most of the time. Chip too, so I kept them busy making up games. Once I was done with my chores, Mrs. Mason was more than happy to let me take them exploring along the path to the pond, looking at the grasshoppers and flowers.

Throughout the morning I had noticed Calvin looking at me. His gaze was uncomfortably penetrating, and I quickly looked away. Each time I caught him looking at me, I wanted to look back again but wouldn't let myself do that. I didn't want to encourage him.

At one point I heard Mr. Mason yell, "Calvin where are you now, boy?"

I looked over in time to see Calvin scowl before his face went blank.

"I'm bringing those two by fours right now, Pa."

I saw him giving the lumber pile a kick as he muttered to himself, but I couldn't make out what he said.

Mr. Mason came around the corner from the backside of the newly-framed barn with a hard look on his face. Calvin was bent over loading the wood into his arms when Mr. Mason raised his hand and knocked him in the back of the head.

"When I say now, boy, I mean now," he growled, "get that lumber around back."

It scared me watching from across the farmyard. I'd never seen such a thing.

The dust started kicking up and I had to turn away. When I looked back Calvin was following his pa with his arms full of lumber. That scene stayed with me.

The day wore on after that. By 3:00 p.m., it was scorching hot and we were all sweating pretty good. I offered to take the three younger children to the pond. It would have been too much for me to take them all swimming, but I knew it would be shady along the bank by the bench and we could squish our toes in the mud along the water's edge. Maybe even wade in just up to our ankles to cool everybody off. I asked Mrs. Mason if it would be okay.

"Why Mary, that is a good idea. It's a hot one for sure and the kids are restless. Let me see if Calvin could go along to help you."

With that, she walked out the door and over to where the barn was quickly taking shape. It seemed strange, even disturbing to me, having the new barn go up in exactly the same place as the old one. It was even the same size, but a little bit taller. I noticed that as I watched her walk away.

She soon came back, "Calvin will be down to the pond shortly to lend a hand," she said coming through the kitchen door.

"Calvin doesn't need to come, Mrs. Mason. I can handle the kids just fine," I said, hoping to avoid being that close to Calvin.

"Nonsense, you have done so much all day and I want him to help out with his brothers and sister."

So off we went down the path, Megan and I holding hands, and Rex and Chip running back and forth across the path in front of us. I picked up Megan a little ways along the path. That grass was high for a toddler.

We all had our shoes and socks off and our pants rolled up, splashing along the edge of the water and having a high time, when Calvin came along. He swooped right in from nowhere and scooped Megan up, running into the water and splashing and twirling her around. At first she giggled and seemed to be having a good time. Then, she got scared when he wouldn't stop.

"Calvin, your ma didn't want us getting all wet. We're just staying along the edge here."

His pants and shirt were soaked, and Megan's pants were too. She started to cry.

"Oh Megan, I thought you'd like this," he said, looking at me. He proceeded to set her down right there in the water where she could barely stand. I ran and snatched her up and took that little girl right back to the grassy edge. I held her and told her it was okay and got her distracted by looking at a ladybug in the grass.

When I looked back toward the water, Calvin had pulled off his shirt and tossed it to shore. He swam out to the middle of the pond, and the boys looked confused about what they should do.

"Rex, Chip," I asked, "would you like to go fishing? You can fish here in the pond and you'll catch plenty too. I know Tommy would like to show you all about that. Let's go back and see how they're doing at the barn and ask Tommy about fishing, okay?"

The boys looked out at Calvin, who was diving down

and swimming in the water. I could tell that Rex was thinking about going out there, and I was determined to get him back up the hill, since he was my responsibility.

"Hey, I think I hear Tommy coming now, you guys. Let's go tell him we want to fish. Grab your shoes and socks and we'll go barefoot."

They went for that and Megan said she was hungry, which was even better. "We can get some cookies too," I said, smiling at them.

I knew Calvin was watching us, even though he was pretending not to. I wanted to get away from there while he was still out in the middle of the pond. I was stunned by his behavior with Megan, making her cry and then putting her in danger by setting her in water that was too deep for her to stand in. It was like he wanted to seem nice, but then he wasn't. I was mad, but I was shaken up too. Confusion and something close to fear mingled inside of me as we headed up the hill.

I hadn't really heard Tommy coming, but I said that to get Rex and Chip's attention. As luck would have it, Tommy was just heading our way as we got up closer to the house. Now, he could join us for milk and cookies. Bessie and Bedelia were back in the milking business, and it was going to taste real good and cold, coming right from the icebox.

Chip and Rex started in on Tommy all at once, "Tommy, Mary says that we can go fishing at the pond. Will you show us how to fish?"

Tommy grinned, "Of course I will. Mary's good at fishing too, you know, so she can help. We only have two poles but we can share. Let's do that another day soon. It's getting late, and I think everyone is about to go home. Your ma wants you to come in now." Tommy scooped up Megan as we went on up to the house.

We came in the door and Mrs. Mason said, "Oh my, Megan, you're all wet. What happened to you?"

I wasn't sure how to handle this. "When Calvin came down, they started playing along the water's edge. I'm so sorry she got wet." I had an uneasy feeling about the whole situation, like I had to be careful not to get Calvin in trouble.

While Mrs. Mason changed Megan's clothes, Dorothy and I packed up the things we had brought. The cleaning was pretty much done, and there were cookies and pitchers of water set on the table for the men. Tommy, Rex, and Chip were playing marbles on the grass under the clothesline and they were all wrapped up in that. Megan came out with her little blankie and sat in a chair on the porch, sucking her thumb. *Poor little thing*, I thought. She looked tired and confused. It had been a big day all around. I didn't see Calvin come back up from the pond.

Chapter Eight

School started in September. The school bus came along our road and stopped partway between Dorothy's house and my farm. Tommy was the first to get picked up and then the bus came to our stop.

I had been worrying about being at the same bus stop as Calvin. I couldn't shake the uneasy feeling I got every time I was around him. He acted nice with the grownups, but I knew better. Dorothy walked with me to the bus stop that first week, which helped a lot. Mrs. Mason walked with her younger kids to the stop while Calvin lagged behind them. He'd run up and get on the bus as soon as it pulled to a stop, saying, "Good morning, Mrs. Freeman," to Dorothy and bye to his ma. That was fine by me, and I could get on the bus and sit with Tommy, ignoring Calvin. But after the first week, Dorothy and Mrs. Mason stopped coming to the stop, and I was the one who started to drag my feet. I didn't want to be alone with Calvin.

It was pretty much the same at school. He was nice to the teacher, and people thought he was a good kid. But he didn't get close to anyone and frequently went off by himself. He did, however, keep finding ways to talk to me alone.

One day, I was outside our classroom by the coat hooks and cubbies, looking for my lunchbox. I knew I'd had it earlier, but it was nowhere to be found.

Tommy was helping me look for it, "I've got to go so I can get to band practice," he said. "I'll share my lunch with you."

"No, you go on. I know I had it and I really want it because Dorothy packed the best stuff today. I'll find it, you go on."

"Okay but hurry. I'll see you later."

I was down on my hands and knees, looking along the floor, through the book bags, when a voice from behind me said, "Are you looking for this?"

Twisting around, I saw Calvin standing there with my lunchbox. It threw me off to be alone in the alcove with him, and he had such a telling look on his face, as though he knew exactly what I was doing.

"Where did you get that?" I said, jumping up and snatching my lunchbox from him.

"I found it out in the hall," he smiled. "Aren't you going to say thank you?"

I just stood there staring at him. "What do you want, Calvin?"

"I thought we could be friends."

"I don't see how. I'm nothing like you."

"Oh, I don't know about that. I admire you, Mary."

"I can't think why," I said as I backed away.

"I heard how you killed your grandpa."

I gasped and backed into the cubbies, hitting my head. I tripped over something on the floor, going down on my knees. He grabbed my wrist to pull me up.

"I just want to know what it was like."

"Don't you dare touch me."

"What's the problem? Why are you all upset?" He seemed to be enjoying this.

"Get away from me. Stay away," I shouted at him and ran off down the hall.

I went into the girl's bathroom, tears running down my face, and hid in one of the stalls. I put my lunchbox on the back of the toilet, lowered the lid and sat on the seat with my feet pulled up so no one could see I was in there, from under the door. Gripped by panic I tucked my head down into my arms, which were circled around my knees. My eyes were closed.

Once my breathing calmed a little and I slowly opened my eyes. I could see through a little space between my feet and there was the blue-green beetle on the floor being very still. That brought them all to me, Momma, Gert, and even Gert's ma who had taught her patience.

"Trust girl, trust yourself."

I lifted up my head, not sure where the voice had come from. I realized that I did trust myself. But I surely did not trust that awful Calvin and I was not going to let him run me off like that again. I hadn't trusted him before and now I knew I had been right. I was going to keep my eyes open and be ready if he ever found me alone like that again.

The bathroom door burst open and a couple of girls came in laughing. I sat still and hoped they'd go away. I heard the water run as they talked about some boy, and then they left. I put my feet back on the floor and noticed that the beetle was gone. As I left the stall, I hoped there was enough time left to eat lunch.

Some weeks later, on a crisp October morning, I was walking slowly down our lane to the bus stop. I could see that the boys were there without Calvin.

"Hi," I said.

Both boys offered a "Hi," and continued kicking a rock back and forth between them. They went on talking as I crossed the road to where the bus always stopped.

"I don't know what he did to her. Pa was so mad. You know there's no messing with Megan."

I heard a truck coming fast from the Masons place. It pulled up near where I was standing.

"Remember what I said. You won't get another chance."

Rex and Chip turned to Calvin as the truck pulled away, but they stayed quiet. Calvin glanced my way, long enough for me to see that his eyes were empty.

Rex said, "Here comes the bus. Get your stuff, Chip."

The boys ran ahead to get on. I was left with a sinking feeling. I couldn't be sure then, but I knew something was terribly wrong with Calvin and his pa. I wanted to tell Tommy but I figured he'd say we should mind our own business.

Tommy was saving a seat for me toward the middle of the bus.

"Hi," I said, sliding in to the seat.

"Hey," Tommy smiled.

I hesitated, then said, "I have to tell you something..."

Calvin came up the steps and boarded the bus, taking a seat at the back. He looked the other way as he passed our seats.

"So what were you going to tell me?"

"I'll tell you later." And to keep him from asking again I switched to asking about homework from the night before. It was easy to get Tommy on to a new subject. He was a great talker, and that came in handy sometimes.

Chapter Nine

The cold of autumn was all around. I had been spending more time in the ravine, and I missed the pond.
Mrs. Mason still asked for help with Megan and Chip
from time to time, but I always made an excuse. I felt
uneasy around Calvin, so avoiding him had become a
habit.

The first Saturday morning in November, I went off
to the ravine as soon as I finished my chores. It was early still, and cold, but the sun was peeking over the hill
by the house and would soon be shining its warmth on
me. I stopped bringing my quilt because it had gotten
a little tear in it, and I didn't want it ruined. Dorothy
showed me how to mend it, but I wanted to keep it safe
all the same.

I had on my old coat and boots, as I sat in a spot
right where the sun came through two trees. I lay back

and listened to the sound of crackling leaves under me, and welcomed the growing warmth on my face. I turned my head to the side and smiled at the big blue-green beetle marching along past my ear. I had looked them up in the encyclopedia at school and knew that it was a Tiger Beetle. *Good name*, I thought. *Gert was like a tiger and these beetles showed up when she did.*

I lifted my head to look around and see if she was there. I jumped. There on the opposite side of the ravine stood Calvin, staring at me.

"What are you doing here?"

"Watching you. Looks like you're enjoying yourself."

"This is my place. You need to leave."

"What, leave now? I just want to talk. I think we do have some things in common."

"No, we don't, now go."

"I'm still waiting for you to tell me how it was for you with your grandpa."

I reached down and picked up the beetle. It felt reassuring in my hand.

"My grandpa dying in that fire was an accident. You've got some messed up ideas that don't have anything to do with me or my grandpa."

"Oh, come on, you don't have to hide from me. I heard about your séances. You're into some stuff I want to know about. Tell me what it felt like knowing you'd killed him."

He had been walking toward me as he talked, down his side of the ravine, across the bottom, and coming up my side. I could feel the beetle moving in my hand. *Trust your instincts.*

I started to back up a little and then stopped myself, "Get out of here."

"What's that in your hand?"

"Nothing."

"Come on, let me see," and he charged those last steps up the hill and grabbed my arm. I jerked away from him, and the beetle flew out of my hand.

"Oh, one of those. What's so special about a bug? Surely, you've got better stuff to mess with." He kicked at it in the grass. "I don't get you, Mary. Why you won't tell me what it was like? That's all I want to know. I think we could have some fun."

"I told you last time never to touch me again! Get out of here or I'll tell your pa that you've been bothering me."

He glared at me as his body went rigid, then turned away, running back down the hill. "We're not done yet," he called back to me.

My eyes followed his progress until he was up and over the other side of the ravine and out of sight. I looked down searching for the beetle, but it was nowhere to be found. Warm air wrapped around me and brought my gaze up. There was Gert. I ran to give her a hug, my arms melting right into her warmth.

"Did you see all of that? He scares me. He thinks that Grandpa and the fire were something that I did on purpose. I feel so bad inside when he's around, heavy and thick like sludge."

"You feel the bad and hurt inside of him."

The beetle crawled up my boot.

"There's something off with that family. Calvin, Megan, their pa...I feel it."

"There are all kinds of people, Mary. Listen to your intuition deep inside. Trust yourself, keep yourself safe, and listen. The answers are always there."

The goose bumps on my arms felt like a premonition.

"Gert, will you please look out for Megan?"

"I think that's a fine idea. I surely will."

With that, she reached over to touch my face and it felt tickly, like a brush of vibrating air. I smiled. She vanished, but I knew she was still near.

Chapter Ten

November was cold which I liked because I could wear my new heavy winter coat. It hung down to my thighs and was a green-and-blue-plaid, wool car coat. I had a green scarf that matched my eyes to go with it and mittens too. It was so much fun to put them on in the morning and wear them to school.

The weekend before Thanksgiving the forecast called for snow. It only took a few inches to make it tough to get around. Dorothy wanted to go to the market early that Saturday morning before the roads got bad. She had a lot of baking to do for Thanksgiving and wanted to get everything in the house that we would need. Cooking and baking had become important to me. I loved the time we spent together making delicious things. Dorothy said I was especially good at rolling dough, and I would burst with pride when she said that.

As we left the house that morning and drove down our lane toward the road, I was considering which five pieces I would choose from the penny candy jars. That was the best thing about going to the market and it was a glorious ritual for me.

Turning right toward town, something caught my eye down the road to the left, toward my old farm. "Dorothy, did you see that?"

"No, what?"

"I think I saw Calvin running across the road with something over his shoulder."

"I didn't see him. Turkeys are in season, maybe he's out hunting with his pa."

"I guess that was it. He always seems so sneaky though..."

Later, returning from town, we turned on the radio and got busy putting everything away. We planned on making two apple pies that day, and Dorothy had me go down to the root cellar and bring up a medium basket of Jonathans for the pies and applesauce.

Humming along while rolling dough, I was smiling at the thought of having only two days of school the coming week. Maddie and her family would be arriving on Wednesday, and I could show off my pie crust.

We were surprised by a knock on the door. It was Tommy's pa.

Dorothy said, "Come in, Tom. You'll catch your death." The snow had started by then.

"Sorry to bother you, Dorothy. Jean Mason called over to our place about an hour ago. I guess your phone's on the blink because she couldn't reach you.

She said they didn't know where Megan had gotten off to. It seems that Jean thought Jeb had taken her to town with him earlier, and Jeb thought she was home with Jean and the boys. When he got home, Jean asked him where Megan was and they realized the neither one of them knew. Rex and Chip thought she had gone to town too. Calvin's not around, so they don't know if she's with him but they don't think so. Have you seen her?"

"No, we haven't. Oh my, Tom, this is awful. Have they checked in the barn? I'm sure the pond is frozen over, so it can't be that…"

"They've looked everywhere, and twice over. A bunch of us have formed a search party and we're all heading out from the Masons' farm. I'll be on my way now." The worry was thick in the creases of his face.

As he went out the door, the shivers running down my back were not from the cold air; it was a knowing that Megan was suffering, cold and alone, or worse.

Twilight descended quickly as the search for Megan began. With the snow coming down thick and fast, the sheriff wanted everyone to stay inside and wait for news. Tommy and his ma were at the Masons helping with the kids. He told me later that the sheriff barked, "We don't need anyone else to go looking for."

Calvin showed up at home just after dark, claiming he didn't know a thing about Megan's whereabouts. He had been their last hope that she was okay. I guess his ma was so distracted with worry that she didn't even ask him about where he'd been. With no phone to get updates, and knowing that men were coming and going with the search, Dorothy got out the big coffee urn and several bags of cookies and rolls from the freezer. She was determined to help in some way, so we loaded everything into the truck and made our way over to the farm. The road was slick, and I was sitting tight to the seat with white knuckles clutching the armrest. The truck slid a little on the downhill section of the farm lane, but Dorothy was good behind the wheel.

We got there and were unloading the coffee and food when Calvin came out the door and walked by us. Tears of fear and confusion sprang to my eyes. An overwhelming sense of sickness oozed into my chest and stomach. I dropped the basket from my hands and stared at Calvin. He turned when the basket tumbled to the ground and our eyes met. I knew instantly. I knew he had done something to Megan.

"What have you done with her, Calvin? Where did you take her?"

He just stared at me. "I don't know what you're talking about. My sister is missing, and I'm going to help look for her." And he took off into the dark.

Dorothy set the coffee urn down and glared at me, "What's gotten into you? That poor boy's sister is missing and you're talking to him like that?"

"Calvin hurt her and took her somewhere, I'm sure of it."

"Your imagination is running away with you, and you've got to stop this, Mary. Calvin is a nice boy. He doesn't deserve to have you talk to him like that." She was stern and looked me square in the face.

Standing there in the snow and cold, I nodded my

head and didn't say another word. I realized again that I was on my own, except maybe for Tommy. No one suspected Calvin and they sure weren't going to listen to me. I would have to find a way to get to Megan.

I turned my eyes back in the direction where Calvin had walked away. I heard the faint sound of a door scraping, drawing my attention to the barn. The light was on over the big door, but dense, falling snow made it hard to see anything.

"Come along now, we need to get these things into the kitchen." I trudged up the stairs behind Dorothy.

Being in the house was overwhelming, like I was in a too bright, too loud place. Having emptied my hands of the box I carried, I turned back toward the door.

"I'll be in the truck," and was out the door before she could say anything.

Tommy had been inside playing with the boys and he came out to sit with me. I told him what had happened with Calvin. Tommy looked at me like he was putting something together and then had his own story to tell.

"Calvin got home just a little while ago. When Mrs. Mason asked him if Megan was with him, he just said no. That was it. No questions, nothing."

"Then he acted put out when supper wasn't ready. Here Megan is missing and he seemed annoyed that his ma hadn't made supper."

"His ma slapped him upside the head. 'Your sister is missing and you're wanting supper?' The boys got all fidgety so I took them into the living room and got them distracted with their Tonka trucks. When I came back to the kitchen, Calvin was gone, and then you and Dorothy walked in."

"You know what I mean, there's something wrong," I paused. "He went into the barn, I'm sure of it. I heard a door scrape. We have to get in there and see what he's up to. There's a flashlight right here in the glove box." The glove box was jammed, but finally came open with a hard yank. "Here it is."

I hopped out the door, turning to whisper to Tommy, but he wasn't following me. I stuck my head back in the truck, "Come on, let's go."

Looking down he said, "I can't. I would get in a heap of trouble with my pa for leaving. I'm supposed to be helping and keeping the kids busy."

"What? Don't you see that Calvin must know what's happened to Megan?"

Pleading, he said, "What can we do? There's a search party and they're going to find her."

"Fine then, I'll go by myself."

"Please don't," he said. "It could be dangerous."

I turned and headed for the barn, the side door seemed best.

"Mary...," Tommy called after me, but I didn't look back.

The snow was deep and I took each step carefully, not wanting to fall or make noise. As I neared the barn door, feeling scared but determined, I lifted the earflap on my cap to listen for sounds from inside, but there was only the quiet of snow falling.

Taking a chance, I flashed the light around for a quick look and saw footprints leading away from the barn toward the woods. He had left. I wasn't sure what to do. Did he have her or was she inside? I went into the barn to see, being careful in case I was wrong and he was in there. I opened the door quietly, stepped just inside and gingerly pulled the door closed. The air was still with an eerie kind of quiet. I'd only been in this new barn once, and it was a lot like our old one. I was naturally drawn toward the loft, moving carefully toward the ladder, keeping the flashlight down so I could see ahead of me. There didn't seem to be anything unusual, but climbing that ladder gave me the creeps. I hadn't been in a loft since the fire. I also didn't know what I was going to find when I got up there.

Reaching the top I peeked over the floor, shining my light around. "Megan," I whispered. "Are you here?"

All I heard was the scurrying of a mouse over to the right. That didn't bother me, and it seemed clear to step up onto the floor. I went left, over toward the haystack.

"Megan, can you hear me?"

There was a window with a little light coming in from outside, and I could see something dark and small on the floor. "Another mouse," I leaned down to check more closely.

It was a mitten, a small one...

Where is she? was my only thought, and my focus to find her took over completely.

I stood with the mitten in my hand and looked around. I could feel myself slip away... as my vision clouded, my thoughts became hazy.

I felt the hand over my mouth, "Megan, shush!"

It was Calvin's voice, harsh but low, like he was

trying to be quiet. I was choking. His hand was over my mouth too tight, and I couldn't breathe. A startled panic ran through me, then nothing.

When I came to, I was on the floor. My cheek was against the floorboards, cold and hurting. I sat up and pulled off my glove, carefully touching my cheek. It was covered with hay dust and blood and throbbed pretty good, too.

My breath caught as I felt a chill penetrate my bones...it was Megan. I had to find her. Getting ahold of myself, knowing I had to stay calm and think, it came to me that the bundle over Calvin's shoulder earlier that day had been Megan. He had taken her somewhere.

My only thought was, *Let her be alive.*

With some effort I got on my feet, gathering my flashlight and wiping my hand on my pants. Then, I scrambled quickly down the ladder, and made my way to the door, opening it slowly. No one could see me.

Calvin's tracks were filling with snow, but I could still make them out well enough to follow. My determination was a powerful force through the deepening snow and difficult terrain. Crossing the road at the same place I'd seen him that morning, I used the flashlight to navigate as I entered the woods, careful not to have it on very much. The men were out looking too, and I didn't want them or Calvin to catch on I that was around.

I tripped and fell on something hard and sharp. The pain shot through my knee, and I got lightheaded. Taking a moment to collect myself, I managed to get up, shake it off and keep going. Though I barely noticed the cold, the snow made it tricky moving over things hiding under the snow. As I progressed, I stopped every few minutes to shine my light around and check for signs of Calvin. Then, I moved on. I repeated this sequence over and over as I continued my one-person search. I heard the men at one point way off to the right, but Calvin seemed to be heading the other way toward the old creek bed.

Time lost all meaning as I felt Megan's lightheadedness and her attempts to pull in air through small gasps. That kept me focused. The snow was letting up a little and the forest was quiet. I thought I saw a light moving up ahead to the left.

It's Calvin. My body tensed.

"Careful girl, think now." It was Gert's voice. I turned off my flashlight and slowed down. As I crept toward the light ahead, I saw Calvin. He was sitting on something, a log or a rock, slumped forward and looking down. He was quite still. I couldn't see real well and the light wasn't on anymore, but his silhouette was clear. I decided to go around wide and get behind him. The snow had stopped, and there was enough moonlight to show me the way. I got in position to see better just as he turned his lantern on. I didn't see any sign of Megan.

He turned around, "Is that you, Mary? Why are you sneaking around? You can come over here by me."

Hesitating, I stood up and shined the flashlight his way.

Working my way toward him, I said, "You told me you were going to look for Megan, but you're not because you already know where she is, don't you?"

He didn't answer. "Show me, so I can see her."

There was a sense of resignation around him. Between that and the quietness of the woods, it was unnerving. I knew he would go along with me, and I could feel he was relieved that I had come.

I noticed the moonlight getting brighter.

He picked up the lantern, "She's just under the rock overhang by the creek bed. I didn't mean to kill her Mary, it was an accident. You know, like your grandpa."

I went numb at his words, but my little voice was telling me to keep going. "I know, you just wanted her to keep quiet." He stood and moved ahead of me. I followed.

"How'd you know that? You weren't watching were you, like with a séance? Is that what happened with your grandpa? Did he figure out about you?"

I knew I had to ignore what he was saying and focus on Megan, "Are we close now?"

The flashlight cast ghostly patterns as I slipped moving along on the hillside.

"Yeah, right here. I slid her up under this rock overhang. Tucked in real good and wrapped in a tarp. I didn't mean to hurt her. She fell and hit her head. I didn't know that would happen."

I could barely breathe. I had come this far but being so close to her…I was getting weak in the knees.

"You'll see. I took good care of her."

I felt a faint but steady beat of hope coming from under that rock.

"Here, hold the lantern. I'll slide her out," he said.

He handed me the lantern. He was so intent on

pulling her out of the hiding spot that he seemed to lose track of everything else. I was petrified at what we were doing, but I knew it was the only way to help her.

Sliding her body out on the slope was awful. Wrapped in the tarp, he had to swing his own body uphill as he pulled so he didn't slide backward. The bundle cleared the rock overhang and came up against the new snow. Calvin pulled harder and got her to the flat area above the rocks.

"Mary, I'll take the lantern now and you unroll her."

I handed him the lantern and set aside my flashlight as I got down next to Megan. There was one rope wrapped around the middle and I untied that first. Then I took hold of the edge of the tarp and started pulling. She rolled slowly over and I worried about hurting her. She was dead weight and stiff.

"You killed her, Calvin." I was crying now and didn't realize it until I heard my voice.

"It was her fault. I had to shut her up with Ma coming in the barn looking for her. Nothing else I could do. She's Pa's little angel. All I wanted was to scare him by keeping her out of sight for a while, like she was lost. Then I would find her and bring her back and he'd think I'd done something good for a change."

I heard his words but could barely comprehend what he was saying. It was too shocking. I was thinking of a TV show I had seen once about a person that seemed to be dead from the cold but was brought back to life. Through all of the commotion inside of me, I still sensed a glimmer of life coming from this bundle.

As I unwrapped the last fold, I could see her arm

sticking out and her hand was kind of bluish white. I was afraid to touch her...

"Go on, girl, trust," I could hear Gert's guidance.

I took ahold of her hand and folded back the tarp to see the rest of her. Hard to imagine there was any life inside that little body.

She had her jacket and little coveralls on. There was dried blood down her face and in her hair, with a cut along her cheek. She was bluish and ghostly looking. I wanted to strike out at Calvin. I stood up and turned to him in a sudden movement and he sidestepped me, "What are you doing?"

"You're sick. Look at what you did!"

"I told you, I didn't mean to."

Anger took over and I swung at him with my flashlight and caught him square in the jaw. He went down hard and I turned back to Megan. I knelt down next to her to check her breathing. I couldn't tell for sure, but with my face right next to hers, I thought I could feel a bit of warm air coming from her nose.

I knew that to save her I would need help. My mind turned to how to get the men to find us. I let out a long, blood-curdling scream, which was followed by a minute of piercing silence. Then I heard voices coming fast.

Calvin looked at me for a long moment, "He's going to kill me," and collapsed into a shaking, sobbing mess.

"Megan's not dead. I feel air coming from her nose. She's breathing. I need you to help me keep her warm. Get up and help me, Calvin."

I scooped her in to my arms, pulling her into me, trying to warm her with my body. I held her with one arm, grabbing for the edge of the tarp to pull around us. "I'll tell them, Calvin. I'll tell them you helped save her and that it was an accident. Come on, I need you to wrap us up."

And then he was there, covering us both with the tarp. We seemed to share one focus, to save Megan. He did his best to put his arms around us too.

In that moment with all three of us wrapped together, I felt overwhelming hope and fear for Megan. That's how they found us moments later—Tommy's pa, the sheriff and some others. Megan's pa was there too and the doctor. It was Doc who got to us first and said, "It's okay, Calvin, you can let go now." They unwrapped the tarp and Doc said, "Mary, let her go. I've got her. I'll take care of her."

I remember it was hard to let her go, as though my arms were locked at the elbows and wouldn't straighten out. Then, Mr. Mason came over looking dazed and confused and let out the loudest, saddest sound I've ever heard. It was a keening sound, something like I'd heard animals make before. That snapped me out of it, and I let Doc take Megan.

"Tom, Sheriff, get your coats off. We're going to wrap her up and get her to the house."

"What happened?" the sheriff was by me now. "We heard a scream. Was that you?"

The adrenalin was wearing off and I barely managed to answer, "Yes."

I looked at Megan; the men had her wrapped up with her pa holding her. He was quieter now with his gaze fixed on her face, his emotions like a storm swirling in his eyes.

Doc said, "I want her back to the house. We need to bring her body temperature up. Time is everything now. Jeb, you carry her. Let's go."

I was looking at Mr. Mason's face, and I'd never seen that look on someone before. His eyes looked like deep, dark holes—so sad, but fiercely determined too. I think he was consumed with a father's need to rescue and protect his young, his little girl. Then I saw Calvin standing way off at the edge of the clearing, just inside the light of all the lanterns. I could see the fear etched on his face, and then he turned and ran.

Mr. Mason, the doctor, and a couple of other men headed back toward the road. Somebody suggested getting a horse for Mr. Mason and Megan, and I think they called on the walkie-talkie back to the farm. The sheriff hoisted me up to his back and insisted on carrying me home.

Chapter Eleven

When we got to the house, Doc had Megan on the kitchen table.

"Jean, warm some water and get all your blankets. Heat the oven and put the blankets in there. We're going to wrap them around Megan. Keep the temperature on a low setting. Everyone else stay clear."

I watched from nearby the stove as Doc pulled open her jacket, unhitched her coveralls, and leaned down with his stethoscope to listen to her chest. It was like time stopped as we waited to see if she was breathing. He put his face close to her nose and felt her wrist, hanging on to it for what seemed like interminable minutes.

"I think we've got something here. Jean, let's get her clothes off, wipe her down with that warm water and cover her up with blankets from the oven. Jeb, lift her carefully. I'm going to lay these quilts down to wrap all the way around Megan. Get any hot water bottles you have, and get those filled and tucked around her too. Dorothy, bring some soap and warm rags to clean this wound."

I watched as they all worked on Megan. Tommy had quietly taken the boys off somewhere else in the house. I stayed in the kitchen, near Megan. I could hear her in my head. It was like she was drifting, like she wasn't there but she was. I felt the need to be close to her, and I edged right in next to the table and touched the side of her face that wasn't hurt. All the rest of her was under the blankets. Doc was cleaning her wound, and I looked at her face. It was still ghostly pale, but I thought maybe a hint of color was coming back.

Straining through her tears, Mrs. Mason said, "Is she going to make it?"

She sounded so frantic and scared. Her baby was lying there on the table, this tiny little girl, so precious and just barely hanging on. I didn't know where Mr. Mason was at that point. It was Doc, Mrs. Mason, Dorothy, and I in the kitchen. I could hear sounds of people talking and moving around outside, and motors running, but my attention remained fixed on Megan. I was aware of what was going on around me, while being in another place, a place of peace and light. It was warm there, with smiling faces and joy that was tangible in the air.

Then I saw Megan, like an angel, illuminating everything with her smile. It was glorious and confusing all at once. Gert said, "Mary, it's alright. She's visiting heaven. It's okay. Just watch."

I saw my Momma then and Gert, standing on the other side of the kitchen by the door to the sitting room. I felt an overwhelming wave of warmth fill the whole space.

Doc said, "Dorothy, check her feet. Are they feeling any warmer? Is the color coming back?"

"Yes, a bit. I think I felt her toes move too."

At that, Mrs. Mason grabbed ahold of Megan's hand, talking to her and calling her, "My precious baby girl."

In a breath she said, "She squeezed my hand! Oh, thank God."

She broke into sobs, leaning her head down and clutching onto Megan. Dorothy let her stay that way for a moment, then moved in next to her and eased her off, telling her she needed to refill the hot water bottles.

Megan's face had still more color as Doc listened to her heart.

"Yes, that's better," he said. "I think it's time to get her to the hospital. Dorothy, get one of the men to warm up my car and put it right here by the door. I think it has the biggest back seat. Jean, get Jeb and tell him to come and carry Megan to the car. On second thought, I'll do that myself."

Gert and Momma had moved on, but I could smell just a bit of Momma's perfume.

Mrs. Mason left the room looking for her husband and I said, "Dorothy, I could see inside of me what had happened to Megan. That's how I was guided to find her. I know you say that's bad and I know people think I'm strange, but I trusted that and we have her back now. I can still feel what's going on inside of her. She's been in heaven, but she came back. I want to stay with her on the way to the hospital. I know she needs me a while longer. Can I go with you too?"

Dorothy looked at me, and then at Doc.

"Mary, I've been around enough sick and dying people to hear stories like this before. I'm going to drive. Dorothy, get Jean, and you get in the car with her to hold Megan in the back seat. Mary, you ride up front with me." He winked, and I knew he understood.

Chapter Twelve

That night, after leaving Megan at the hospital, Mr. Mason went looking for Calvin. He expected to find him back at the house, but he wasn't there. In fact, he never came back at all.

On a shining Saturday afternoon early that next spring, I was winding my way to my special place. Making my way up the hill from the bottom of the ravine, I saw something swinging in the breeze from a limb, angled to make an offering. It was a paper bag. Inside was a little stick figure doll and a note.

"Dear Mary,
    Will you give this to Megan? I can't come around to do it myself. Pa never did want me, and I suppose he's glad I'm gone now. He was always calling me a little bastard when he'd take

me out back of the barn and let me have it. You see, Ma was already expecting me before she met Pa, and he made it clear that I was born from no good. Never could do anything right for him. Seems better that I be on my own now.

Thank you for helping that night with Megan. I wish we could have been friends. Calvin"

Epilogue

As with so much of life, there are all kinds of times—hard, good, confusing, and sometimes scary. Through it all, we are best served by listening quietly to that knowing deep inside. And, of course, we must always trust ourselves. I learned that back then, during the time following my grandpa's death, and it's been a part of me ever since. The night we saved Megan, I listened to myself and it made all the difference.

As I sat cross-legged in the ravine, offering my face up to the sun, I thought about those long-ago events, and I smiled as appreciation for life filled me up. *No matter what comes, things work out and the good always comes again. Sometimes you just have to wait.*

"I heard that girl, and you are right."

Smiling, I turned toward Gert, who was sitting on the big rock behind me.

"You surprised me!"

"You've been busy. What with Tommy and your babies, you've got your hands full. A good kind of full."

I chimed in, "Then there's Megan's wedding to get ready for too. And the farm doesn't run itself. Thank goodness Dorothy is over so much to help with the kids. Yes, it's definitely busy these days." I was still smiling.

"Come over by me, Mary. I've got something to say."

She was the boss, plain and simple. I chuckled at that as I settled close to her.

"You know I haven't been around as much lately... I'm going to be taking my leave soon. After all, there's only so much an old gal can give."

She went on, "You have grown into a wise woman, a lot like me in fact."

That grin could turn my day around. I beamed at her.

"You will keep teaching those around you, as I have taught you, and I can go on now and rest."

I guess I wasn't surprised, but I felt melancholy all the same.

Gert continued, "Whenever you have anything to figure out, or to get over, or do better with, you know where to look for your answers. No matter how things seem, or what others say, trust yourself girl. It works every time."

And it does, every time. My life is precious to me, full of love for my family, both here and the ones who come to visit from time to time. That time long ago, when I was wondering about who I belonged to, well, turns out I belong mostly to myself. Took a lot of love from those around me to help me learn that.

I leaned in for one of those hugs that I cherish, all light and airy, warm and reassuring. I'd come to feel whole on my own, but I saved up Gert's hugs in a special place where I could go when I needed a little extra comfort.

Author's Note

I wanted to tell this story as a way of illustrating that loving kindness, caring, and patience heal and grow healthy children. They learn to trust themselves and develop the strength to live life on their own terms.

Thank you for reading *Growing Home,*
Jane S. Schreiner

Made in the USA
Middletown, DE
03 January 2017

39036391R00083